Pride Publishing books by Megan Linden:

Harrington Hills
Leading Me Home
Building a Home

I0542120

HARRINGTON HILLS
Volume One

Leading Me Home

Building a Home

MEGAN LINDEN

Harrington Hills Volume One
ISBN # 978-1-78686-059-0
©Copyright Megan Linden 2016
Cover Art by Posh Gosh ©Copyright October 2016
Interior text design by Claire Siemaszkiewicz
Pride Publishing

Published in 2016 by Pride Publishing, Newland House, The Point, Weaver Road, Lincoln, LN6 3QN, United Kingdom.

LEADING ME HOME

Dedication

For Agnieszka, who loves werewolves even more than
I do.

Chapter One

Two weeks into his unemployment, Kevin was yet to regret being fired. His sleep schedule was finally somewhat stable and he enjoyed being at home every night, where his main task was to catch up on all the shows he'd missed when he was tending the bar.

He was about to reach for the last slice of leftover pizza when he heard knocking on the door. The familiar signal—two quick knocks followed by two more after a short pause—meant Kevin already knew who was outside.

"Everything's all right?" he asked as he opened the door and let Taylor in. They'd lived next to each other for over a year and a half now, and they regularly dropped by each other's places at various hours of the day, but five to midnight was pretty late, even for them. "Aren't you supposed to be buried under the deadlines?"

"Two projects down, one to go." Taylor flopped down onto the couch and grabbed the last slice of pizza. "It's cold," he said, scrunching his nose, but that didn't stop him from taking a bite.

"No one forces you to eat it." Kevin rolled his eyes and sat down in his place on the couch. "What's up? Deadline jitters?" He'd witnessed it happen countless of times by now. There was always a point when the stress of running time hinged on the threshold of a nervous breakdown and Taylor's manic energy had to get out somehow. The fastest way to deal with it would be to change and run as a wolf, but they were living in the middle of a city not really known for its wolf population, so that option was rarely on the table.

"I got a call from home." Taylor burrowed deeper into the couch cushions and Kevin was sure that even if he weren't a werewolf, he would be able to sense Taylor's unease. "Mom A has informed me that if I come to the wedding alone, she will stage an intervention—in the form of presenting me to all eligible bachelors from our pack."

Kevin told himself that the sudden roll in his stomach came from too much pizza and a reaction to Taylor's stress. It was most certainly not from anything even remotely close to jealousy at the thought of a bunch of men fighting for Taylor's attention. He put his feet on the coffee table slowly. "Isn't she going to be too busy with the wedding?"

Taylor finished chewing another bite before speaking again. "She'll never be too busy to try to bully me into dating."

"Lovely," Kevin muttered. He knew she was both Taylor's mom and his pack's Alpha, but there should be some limits.

"I need to find someone to go with me." Taylor stared at the ceiling. "Who do we know that could do this?"

Kevin shook his head. "Stop it. It's insane."

"Most of my friends are taken, damn it," Taylor continued as if he hadn't heard him and Kevin wondered if there was even any point in trying to reason with the crazy person his best friend obviously was.

"You don't need a date," he tried one more time.

"Yes, I do. You don't know my mother."

Kevin sighed. "Listen, I get that you want to make your mother happy. She's your mom. She's your Alpha. I get it. But you don't have to do everything she wants you to do." He'd heard a lot of stories about Taylor's family and pack, and they all seemed nice. It was obvious Taylor cared about them. But sometimes it seemed like he didn't see anything else. "It's just a wedding. You're allowed to go alone."

"I don't want to go alone if I have to endure my mother's terrible attempts at setting me up." Taylor winced. "She tried once, when I was in high school. Let's just say it didn't end up well."

"You're not in high school anymore!"

Taylor shrugged. "I still don't want to risk it." Then he sat up straight. "Wait, you're free! You can come with me! That's it, that's the solution."

Kevin gaped at him for a moment, frozen in place. *What the hell?* "No, it's not the solution! Just tell her no, Taylor."

But his friend was already on the roll. "I mean, I thought about it before, back when I got the invitation, but there was no way Sotto would let you go for two weeks to attend a wedding, so I didn't say anything," Taylor went on.

Kevin wanted to bare his teeth at the mention of his asshole ex-boss. Looking back, he had no idea how he'd lasted five months at the bar.

"But you don't have a job anymore and you're not doing anything… It's perfect!"

Kevin couldn't hold back a snort. He'd come to terms months ago with the fact that he found Taylor's bluntness somehow charming. It was just more proof of his Taylor-related insanity. He sure didn't think clearly around this guy.

"We'll agree to disagree on that," he said, but Taylor hardly noticed.

"Come on… You can't say no to two weeks of free vacation. I'll pay for the tickets and we'll stay at my family house." He nudged him in the thigh. "Free food, free drinks and gorgeous sights for you to take hundreds of photos of. You know you want to."

What Kevin knew was how much trouble that could get him in. Sure, a part of him wanted to do it, pretend for a bit to be Taylor's boyfriend and enjoy it while it lasted, but it would be too easy to get lost in the lie. Kevin often told himself that he still wasn't in too deep with Taylor and he could handle his crush. Trying it for show could push him over the edge into the Land of Heartbreak, a place he had been fighting for over a year not to end up in.

"This is not a good idea," he told Taylor when he realized he hadn't said anything for too long.

Taylor frowned. "Why not?"

"Because your pack knows about me?" Kevin tried to reason with him. "I've heard you telling them more than once that we hang out. They know we're friends and they will see right through the lie."

"We'll tell them we only recently decided to try dating."

I wish, the voice at the back of Kevin's head whispered, but he ignored it. "They won't buy it."

"Why not? Two friends, both gay and single, decide they want to take their friendship a step further."

Taylor shrugged. "Tell me that doesn't sound like about a third of the couples you know."

Kevin took his feet off the coffee table and put them back on the ground, leaning forward to rest his forearms on his thighs. "Yeah. It may work when it's real. This wouldn't be."

"Which they won't know!"

Kevin shook his head. "Until they find out."

"How exactly?" Taylor asked him. "We know each other well and we smell like each other already from all the time we spent together." He shrugged again. "No one expects PDAs. So unless you're planning to uncover our plan to them yourself, I don't see how they could find out."

Kevin rubbed his left ear. He hated when Taylor did that. He had a talent of presenting even a truly terrible idea in a way that made it seem plausible—or even good. He should have become a lawyer, not a web designer. "I don't think—"

Taylor leaned in closer and clasped his hand over Kevin's forearm. "Please, Kev. Two weeks, that's all I ask."

You have no idea what you're asking, Kevin thought, but kept his mouth shut. He couldn't tell Taylor the biggest issue he had with this plan, because he didn't want his best friend to ever find out about his feelings.

He opened his mouth to say no anyway, because even without his crush, this whole thing was a terrible idea. But when he looked up, Taylor's wide gray eyes staring at Kevin from close distance made the refusal impossible. He sighed. He was so screwed. "Two weeks," he said, rubbing his ear again. "And we're setting up some rules. We need backstories and such."

Taylor grinned and tightened his grip on Kevin's forearm before letting go. "We'll just change a few things from our real lives and we'll be fine."

No, Kevin thought, looking down on the coffee table. *I don't think we will.* It was a disaster waiting to happen.

"Okay," he made himself say instead, trying to keep the worst case scenarios away, at least for now. He was pretty sure he was going to freak out after Taylor went back to his place.

"Thanks, man." Taylor's smile turned soft when Kevin glanced up at him. "I really appreciate it."

Kevin lowered his eyes again.

I'm so screwed.

Chapter Two

When they were waiting to board the plane, Taylor once again marveled over the fact that they were actually going to do this. They were heading to Harrington Hills. He not only had his mothers off his back, but he would also get to show Kevin his hometown and pack.

He looked over at the guy. Kevin was reading from his phone, slouching in the plastic chair next to him.

He was the first friend Taylor had ever made outside the pack. Everything had been weird back when he'd first come to San Francisco—new city, new job, being alone and away from the pack. Being on his own had been the point of the move, but Taylor hadn't fully realized before how weird and uncomfortable it was going to be. His first evening in the city, he'd been practically vibrating with tension and he'd finally decided to go for a run after a long day of unpacking. When he'd had opened the door and stepped outside, the sense of relief was instantaneous. Then the smell of another wolf had hit Taylor hard in the chest and he'd almost taken a step back when he'd seen a guy coming out from the apartment next to his. The memory of *wolf-familiar-no-other-but-still-familiar* had faded over time, but Taylor still remembered how it had helped him relax for the first time since he'd gotten there. He hadn't been alone anymore.

It had taken them a few weeks to exchange more than a nod and hello, but after they'd started talking, they'd fallen into it as if they'd known each other for a long time. Being away from his pack had gotten easier after that.

And now Taylor had the opportunity to introduce Kevin to his family and to show him his home. He didn't realize he was grinning until Kevin elbowed him.

"Hey, dial down your smile or someone will faint," he teased. "What's up with you?"

Taylor didn't even try to contain his enthusiasm. "I'm going home."

Kevin stared at him for a few seconds longer, like he was waiting for the rest of the reason, but then he nodded and went back to his phone. Taylor looked away, pretending to study the list of upcoming departures on the screen hanging on the wall on his right. He knew Kevin didn't really understand it, didn't get having a close-knitted family and pack. They had never talked about hows and whys, but he knew Kevin was a lone wolf. No pack affiliation, no family members — human or wolf. Kevin seemed fine with it, but Taylor couldn't even imagine living like that. For him, leaving his hometown had always been temporary. It had been a challenge, a traditional way to hone his power and skills — a rite of passage of sorts. He had always known he was going back — to his pack, to his family — to take his rightful place as the Alpha's Son.

The male voice announced over speakers that the boarding for their plane was about to start and it dragged Taylor back to the present.

"Are you sure I know everything I need to know?" Kevin asked as they joined the boarding line.

Taylor thought through all the things they had come up with in the last few days. Most of the stuff his potential partner should know were things they had already learned about each other. Taylor had talked about his pack so much that Kevin knew basically everything there was to know about it.

As they moved to the front of the line, Taylor handed the gate agent his ticket. "I think so."

Kevin nodded as he handed his as well. "Any past relationships that can come back to bite you in the ass? Or me?"

The agent looked up, alarmed, probably thinking Kevin was talking to her. Taylor chuckled.

"I dated some, but I've never gotten serious with anyone, so no drama," he said, turning to Kevin, and noticed from the corner of his eye how the agent relaxed. She handed the tickets back with a smile and let them pass.

"Good." Kevin adjusted the strap of his camera bag swung over his shoulder. "I've seen movies that went like this and I wouldn't like to end up with a black eye or something."

Taylor raised his eyebrows, amused. "You've seen movies like this?"

Kevin rolled his eyes at him. "'I dated some'," he parroted. "This kind of story is date movie material."

"Never seen one like it."

"What do you do on— Wait, no." Kevin raised his hand to stop him when Taylor opened his mouth. "I don't want to know." His ears turned red and Taylor burst out laughing.

"No, this is good. This is important." When Kevin shot him a glare, he smirked. "We need to discuss what we did on our dates, so we don't get caught."

Kevin frowned. "Your family will demand details?"

"If you mean the sexual details, then no." Taylor hesitated as they were entering the plane. "Well, maybe aside from Tia, Mom A's niece. She likes to cause trouble and embarrass her siblings and cousins. But other than her, no, no sex-related questions. General 'what do you do' will definitely come up, though."

When they found their seats, Taylor let Kevin have the window seat and sat down next to him. He rolled his head to try to relax his stiff neck. The nerve endings along his entire spine were tingling. His wolf didn't like to fly. Taylor hid his hands under the folded jacket on his lap and let his claws out to release some of the tension.

"Then we'll just tell them the truth," Kevin said, looking like he was perfectly fine traveling in the air.

Taylor rolled his neck again and tried to stop thinking about flying and focus on their conversation. "Yeah, okay," he said in the end. When they were hanging out, they usually went running or played tennis, or — when they stayed inside — gorged on pizza and played on Taylor's old PlayStation. They could also spend hours watching any crime show available and trying to come up with bizarre stories of what could have happened. Every one of those things was pretty good date material, in Taylor's opinion. Nobody was going to question it.

He opened and closed his fists under the jacket and realized the claws were gone. Apparently he'd just needed a good distraction. Another thing that probably helped was the familiar scent. He was wearing Kevin's oversized T-shirt under his shirt while Kevin had Taylor's old hoodie on. They'd done it to mix their scents more for the sake of Taylor's pack, but it turned out that right now it was helping Taylor as well. When he concentrated and tuned out other smells, it was just the two of them sitting next to each other like a hundred times before. Taylor could pretend he was home.

* * * *

Taylor located Mom B and Zack almost immediately after he and Kevin stepped into the baggage claim area, since Zack was hovering over pretty much everyone, with his six foot four frame and body of a football player. Taylor pointed both him and his mom to Kevin.

"There they are," he said, leaning closer to Kevin as someone bumped into him from behind.

"The deputy sheriff is Zack, right?" Kevin asked, noticing the uniform.

"Yeah." Taylor still had trouble imagining his cousin as a respectable officer of the law. He remembered way too many times when Zack would get into trouble as a teenager. "And that's Mom B next to him."

He grabbed Kevin's elbow to steer him toward his pack members. Taylor suddenly realized how at ease he felt already, how tension just seemed to abandon him when he saw his pack in the flesh, when his wolf sensed his family. He quickened his pace.

"Taylor!" His mom dragged him down into a hug and he fitted his face into her neck with a relieved huff. Home. Security. Love. They nuzzled each other's necks for a minute and she scraped him lightly at the back of his neck. He bit down a sigh. "Welcome home, honey."

"Thanks, Mom." His voice was muffled before he pulled away. The tension coming off Kevin next to him helped Taylor remember where they were and get a grip. He exchanged a quick nod and a hug with Zack before turning to Kevin. "Mom, this is Kevin Wallace. Kevin, this is my mom and the Beta of the Harrington Pack, Theresa Harrington."

Taylor had a split moment of panic wondering if Kevin had ever met a pack leader before, if he knew the rules. Harrington Pack wasn't strict about them, but only for the insiders. The outsiders had to behave in certain ways if they didn't want to cause trouble. He called himself a moron for forgetting it right as Kevin nodded to his mom, slightly tilting his head. Enough to show respect, but not surrender. Taylor relaxed and his mom grinned, nodding back before she extended a hand.

"It's so nice to meet you."

Kevin smiled as they clasped hands. "You too, Beta. I've heard great things about you and your pack."

"Taylor spoke highly of you as well," his mom said and Taylor nudged him in the side.

"Don't let it go to your head," he teased Kevin before introducing him to Zack. They nodded and shook hands, but no one bared his throat to anybody since they recognized themselves as equals. Taylor wondered briefly where Kevin had learned the proper protocol.

"Oh, you definitely should let it go to your head." Taylor's mom picked the conversation right up after, grinning at Kevin once again. "Taylor told us you're handsome after the first time you'd met."

Taylor groaned and Kevin raised his eyebrows at him. "You did?"

"I mentioned you and they asked," Taylor told him, hoping he wasn't blushing. It wasn't a big deal. Everyone could see Kevin was handsome, with his dark eyes, almost black hair, and his slender body. Taylor didn't have to be ashamed for stating the obvious.

"Way to lose whatever points that could've gotten you," his mom said before throwing Kevin a knowing look. Zack chuckled, glancing between them, and Taylor stared at her. She wasn't usually like that with outsiders. She was a warm person, yes, but reserved until she considered someone one of their own. With Kevin, she seemed to jump right into the familiar treatment.

"He's quite used to losing his points," Kevin told her before smirking at Taylor. "And by now I know him too well to be surprised."

"Hey, I do nice things for you," Taylor argued. It wasn't even a lie. He helped Kevin move his furniture around every few months, had fixed his sink once and he'd shared his PlayStation with him numerous times.

"Speaking of things," Kevin said, looking at the baggage line. "I should go pick up my suitcase. Please excuse me. It will only be a few minutes, hopefully," he addressed Taylor's mom before turning to him and handing him his camera bag. "Be careful with it."

"I will. I know how you get about your babies," Taylor said, carefully putting it over his shoulder. He got a smack on his other shoulder for that then he watched Kevin as he went to pick up his baggage.

"You don't have anything there?" Zack asked, but Taylor shook his head and pointed at his small backpack without taking his eyes off Kevin.

"I packed lightly, since I have a lot of stuff at home. And Kevin has my tux in his suitcase."

"I like him already," his mom said and Taylor turned to her. She was smiling softly at him and his wolf preened under his mother's warm attention. He missed this more than he'd realized. "You sure as hell took your time, but turns out you know how to pick them, in the end."

He felt a pang in his chest at that. Taylor hadn't doubted his decision to bring Kevin before, but now he could see the downside of this whole thing. He had known his pack would like Kevin, of course, but he hadn't considered what would happen if they liked him too much. He hadn't thought about the fallout of their eventual 'breakup'.

"I'm glad you like him," he said in the end. When Kevin retrieved his suitcase from the line and turned to smile at him, Taylor made himself smile back. *It will be fine*, he told himself. *Everything will be fine.*

Chapter Three

After a good start with Taylor's mom, he gave himself a firm talking-to while he was waiting to retrieve his suitcase. For now, everything seemed to be going well, so Kevin just had to be himself, only more into Taylor. *Well, more openly into Taylor.* He had to balance the act of simultaneously lowering his guard enough to show his true feelings, and raising his guard to avoid letting this whole thing get to him too much before it came to an end. Because it was going to end and the one thing Kevin had to be especially careful about was to not leave Taylor's hometown with his heart broken. An unrequited crush he could handle, but letting himself believe it — *they* — could be real would just end horribly for him.

After he finally took hold of his suitcase and rejoined Taylor, his mom and Zack, Kevin was ready to play his part and the small talk in the car came easily. The ride from the airport to Harrington Hills helped to relax Kevin.

Taylor had told him about his childhood home a little bit, but the big house on the outskirts of the forest was more beautiful than Kevin had imagined. Two stories in the main part, lower wings on both sides, a big porch and the wide driveway on the left side — all of it seemed to fit seamlessly into the encompassing forest. The wall of trees on the right was like an extension of the house, just like the house seemed to be an extension of the forest. Kevin was already itching to spend hours out here, taking photos of the area from various vantage points and in different light.

"Kevin's silent and almost gnawing at his camera bag. That's the best compliment you can get," Taylor told his mom and Zack, dragging Kevin out of considering filters for the afternoon shots.

"What?" He turned to his supposed boyfriend who smirked and reached out to catch Kevin's hand that was apparently playing with one of his camera bag's many zippers. *Huh.* Kevin could feel himself blush, hoping that the others would interpret it as the embarrassment over Taylor's words, not over the way Taylor was holding his hand. Kevin's fingers twitched in his grip and Taylor let him go as the car came to a stop.

"We would love for you to take photos of this place," Taylor's mom told him, turning in her front seat to smile at him. "Taylor showed us some of your work. It's beautiful."

Kevin blinked. Taylor hadn't mentioned anything about that.

"Busted." Taylor at least looked sheepish about it. "I admit that I wanted to show you off."

Kevin nodded. It wasn't something a boyfriend could have a reason to be upset about and it wasn't like Kevin really had a problem with it. He just didn't expect it. That was all.

"I will make sure to give you some," he finally said to Taylor's mom. "If you want something specific, though, let me know."

She grinned. "Thank you."

By the time they left the car, there was a small gathering at the front steps of the house. The tall woman in the middle of the crowd was obviously the Alpha of the pack, Taylor's 'Mom A'.

'I needed some way to differentiate them as a kid and I didn't want to call them Mom One and Mom Two,' Taylor had explained it to him a few months ago, after Kevin had overheard him talking on the phone. *'Coming up with Mom A and Mom B after the Alpha and the Beta of the pack was probably the most brilliant thing I've ever thought of. At least I thought so as a kid. But it stuck.'*

As they came closer, he could see the familiar resemblance between the Alpha and Taylor. The nose and eyes, the dark hair and impressive height—there was no question those two were related.

Kevin stopped about ten feet from the steps and nodded, slightly tilting his head, the same way he had at the airport. He might have not grown up as a part of any pack, but he'd spent a lot of time around one and knew werewolf customs very well. Keep the distance from the Alpha. Bare your neck. Control your heart and never show fear. Wait for the Alpha to address you first.

Taylor stopped by his side and mirrored his posture while both the Beta and Zack moved closer to the group on the steps. Zack nodded at the Alpha and stood aside while the Beta came up to stand right before her mate. The Alpha looked at her as she put her hand on the side of the Beta's neck. She nodded at whatever she saw in her eyes and the Beta stepped up to stand at her side.

Then the Alpha moved forward. "As the Alpha of the Harrington Pack, I welcome you on the Pack's land," she said and her voice seemed to move like a wave through Kevin. She was more powerful than Taylor had let on and that made Kevin's wolf anxious.

Never show fear, he reminded himself. *You are not an enemy.*

"Thank you for allowing me to join you at this time of celebration." The well-rehearsed, standard words fell out of his mouth. He could recite all the ceremonial speeches in his sleep, but it had been a long, long time since he'd had to use that particular knowledge.

"Hi, Mom," Taylor said next to him and Kevin had to bite the inside of his cheek to not burst out laughing. The bizarre counterbalance of their greetings seemed very funny to him.

Luckily, he wasn't the only one. He could see the Beta's lips twitch and the Alpha nodded and relaxed, smiling crookedly at her son.

"Come here, both of you."

Kevin watched as Taylor hugged and nuzzled with his mom just like he had with the other one earlier, and he waited his turn. Then he shook the Alpha's hand and held her gaze as she assessed him. He realized he wasn't afraid of her as an Alpha—after spending most of his life as a lone wolf, the werewolf hierarchy didn't faze him. It was like a game that, if you knew the rules, you could almost never lose. But Kevin was anxious about her as Jolene Harrington, Taylor's mom. He wanted her to like him. Even if all of this—him and Taylor—was not real, Kevin still wanted, for reasons he chose not to examine too closely, to gain her approval.

"I look forward to getting to know you better," she said after a moment and he nodded.

"I look forward to it as well," he answered. Kevin thought she seemed both curious and wary, and he couldn't blame her at all. Taylor was not only her son, he was the Alpha's Son, the werewolf that would one day rule her pack, and a few weeks earlier he'd been single. She had every right to be suspicious. *I'm not the one who came up with the master plan*, Kevin imagined telling her. *And I'm only following it because it was your son who asked.*

After that, the introductions and greetings seemed to go on forever, but Taylor never left his side. Kevin tried to memorize as many names as possible, but it was impossible for him to remember them all at once. He would just make Taylor draw him a diagram or something later. There were a few people who Kevin knew he had to never get wrong, though. One of them was Elijah, the Beta's father, who narrowed his eyes at him and looked him up and down without saying a word. *Charming*, Kevin thought. Another important person was Paul, one of the cousins, who seemed to hold a grudge against Taylor. It was subtle, but Kevin easily picked up on it—the posturing, the tightness in the shoulders. He had seen before how some of the men calling themselves alpha males reacted to Taylor. Luckily it didn't seem likely to end up in a bar fight this time around.

Jack and Julia, the twins and Taylor's younger siblings, apparently missed their oldest brother very much, seeing as they jumped him as soon as the most senior members of the pack had greeted both Taylor and Kevin. Literally jumped him. Kevin stared at the three of them, amazed how Taylor had no problems holding up Julia who was at his front, and Jack, who draped himself over Taylor's back. Seeing Taylor presenting his strength easily like that made Kevin want to bare his neck and surrender. It was nothing like a show of respect for the heads of the pack. It was primal and heavy, and holding it back was hard enough to make him sweat under his T-shirt. Smelling Taylor's scent on him and on the hoodie didn't make controlling himself any easier.

Kevin looked away and found the Beta watching him. He could feel himself blush and hoped she would take it as a sign of nerves, not... On the other hand, he was supposedly Taylor's boyfriend. Sexual attraction was to be expected.

"Kev, hey, come here," Taylor said after the twins climbed off him and he put his arm around Kevin's shoulders and brought him closer. Kevin was pretty much plastered to his side now. He hesitated for a moment, but then he put his arm around Taylor's waist. "These are Julia and Jack, the Terrible Two."

The twins exchanged handshakes with him and smirked.

"Our brother with a boyfriend," Jack drawled. "Who would've thought?"

"You make it sound like I'm against relationships." Taylor rolled his eyes.

Kevin looked up at him with raised eyebrows. "Did you even go out with someone twice since you've come to San Francisco?" He wouldn't call Taylor a player — he went out too little for it to count — but as far as Kevin knew, he had nothing more than one-night stands through all this time.

Taylor frowned as if he was trying to remember. "No, but that's just because I knew they wouldn't be right."

Why was that? Kevin wanted to ask, but in their current situation it would look like he was fishing for compliments and reassurance, so he kept his mouth shut.

Julia didn't, though. "For the Moon's sake, you are *old*. Dating doesn't mean you declare someone your mate."

"I don't want to waste my time and somebody else's, if it isn't going to work out anyway," Taylor said, sounding like it should be obvious to everyone.

"Does it mean Kevin here is your mate?" Jack asked, looking between them, and Kevin stilled. Taylor tensed as well, the muscles beneath Kevin's arm suddenly taunt. It wasn't a question someone should just blurt out like that.

Julia elbowed her twin. "Jack, shut up."

"Sorry," the guy muttered and looked down on the ground. "That was out of line."

No arguments here. It wasn't just this particular situation—pretend relationship and the fallout that would surely follow later on—it was a general rule. Mating was intimate and it wasn't something anybody should ask about unless they were approached.

Taylor nodded. "You know better." He managed to sound both chastising and supportive, and Kevin glanced up at him again. He continued to discover a different side of Taylor since they got here and it was fascinating.

"I do." Jack kept his head down. "My apologies to both of you."

Kevin waited for Taylor to react since it was his home and his pack.

"I accept," the future Alpha said before turning to Kevin, who nodded and repeated the words to Jack. After that, the tension seemed to break and Taylor smirked as he reached out to mess Jack's hair.

The brothers were in a friendly shoving match by the time the Alpha spoke up from the porch.

"The supper will be ready in twenty minutes."

Taylor let go of Jack and looked at Kevin. "We should probably go freshen up a bit."

"Dibs on the shower!" Kevin announced and smirked at Taylor who rolled his eyes.

"You're twelve."

* * * *

Kevin sat down on the big bed in Taylor's room with a relieved sigh. His shower was very short, but it was enough to get rid of a tension headache and his energy went up after he washed off the flight and the rollercoaster of emotions afterward. When he heard the shower turning on again, he got up, dropped the towel and reached for his suitcase. He put their tuxes aside, draping them over the armchair. Taylor could put them in the closet later, but Kevin didn't want to overstep his boundaries.

It's completely different than in San Francisco, he realized as he pulled out a long-sleeved shirt and dark gray jeans. Back at home, Taylor's apartment was almost like his own. He wouldn't hesitate to put stuff in Taylor's closet there—or pull them out, for that matter. Last winter, he'd grabbed an additional blanket from one of the closets almost every time he'd been over, since Taylor was a freak who always ran hot and didn't bother with heating much. Kevin, on the other hand, would gladly cocoon himself in blankets and stayed like that from late October to mid-March every year.

The shower cutting off brought Kevin to the present. He quickly put on his clothes and searched for the socks next, so by the time Taylor came out, shirtless and in a towel—the world was either testing Kevin or punishing him for some past sins — he was dressed and ready.

"How are you holding up?" Taylor asked as he opened his closet. He was turned away from the bed, so Kevin was able to stare freely at his back, tracing the lines of the muscle and the water lines from Taylor's wet hair that was glued to the back of his neck.

He took a deep breath. "So far, so good," he said, turning away from the sight that made his mouth water. "And you were right. This place truly is beautiful."

Taylor sent him a pleased smile from behind his shoulder. "I will take you on a tour. You haven't seen half of it."

"Great, I'm in." Kevin nodded. "And how about you, how are you doing?"

"I'm fine. No one seems to suspect anything and they seem happy." Taylor shrugged. "And I can enjoy just being home, without people nagging me about being single all the time."

"Yeah."

Kevin got busy with his phone, giving Taylor some privacy to get dressed, and he was idly browsing his Instagram feed until Taylor moved to stand in front of him. He was dressed in black jeans and black T-shirt and his dark hair was falling into his eyes. Calling him 'hot' wouldn't come close to giving him justice.

"So, here's a thing," Taylor started and Kevin's stomach did a somersault.

"What is it?" He put his phone away. They should be going in a minute if they didn't want to be late, but whatever Taylor wanted, it seemed important.

"I know it's not…easy and we can think of something else, if you want to say no, because you totally can, of course —"

"Spit it out, Taylor."

"May I scent you?"

Kevin could feel his eyes going wide and he clutched hard the bedcover he was sitting on. The wolf in him chanted *yesyesyes*, but his mind was telling him to run.

But really, his answer couldn't be anything else than, "Yes."

Taylor's nostrils flared. "You sure? We agreed on the clothes and stuff and I thought it would be enough, but being here... All those smells are fucking with me."

"We need to smell like each other," Kevin said a little breathlessly. "Since you're the future Alpha, *I* need to smell like *you*."

He got up slowly. There were mere inches between them now and the air was suddenly hot and dry. They'd never done this, not like this. Hugging, sharing space and things, yes. But this? This was different. Kevin closed his eyes as he tilted his head, exposing his neck, and he heard Taylor's sharp inhale.

Do it already, Kevin wanted to tell him. Something was trembling inside him and he felt as if his body were going to shatter any second.

The first touch of Taylor's nose against the open skin of his neck made Kevin freeze and Taylor paused. Kevin huffed and tilted his shoulder a little up, pushing his body closer to Taylor. The shuddering inhale against his skin made Kevin reach out blindly and rest his hands on Taylor's hips. His whole neck and shoulder were tingling as Taylor nosed the skin, leaving his scent where it should be, if they were —

If they were something different. Kevin squeezed his eyes shut and let go of Taylor's hips. *It's just for show*, he reminded himself. He ignored the goosebumps he could feel on his skin as he took a step back.

Taylor's eyes were glazed over with pupils blown wide enough the usual gray was barely visible. His nostrils flared and he leaned forward a fraction as if he wanted to follow Kevin before he stopped himself and blinked rapidly a few times.

Kevin didn't know what to say to break the awkward silence. He wanted to reach up and touch his neck, touch the skin Taylor had just been marking. He didn't. He shoved his hands into his pockets and turned his head to stare at the wall on his right.

"We should probably go." His voice seemed alien to his own ears, but that might have been because his pounding heart was deafening everything else.

Taylor didn't say anything for a long while and Kevin fought with himself not to look at him. He couldn't meet his eyes right now.

"We should," Taylor said in the end and turned away. They pocketed their phones in silence and left the room.

Chapter Four

Taylor wouldn't be able to tell anyone what happened during the first half an hour of the dinner. He couldn't concentrate on anything anybody said and he wasn't sure if whatever he was saying made any kind of sense. All he was able to think of — to smell — was Kevin. He had never had such a strong reaction to scenting someone and he had no idea what happened. Taylor tried to remember the last time he'd nuzzled somebody outside the pack, but he couldn't come up with anything. Surely he'd scented someone during sex, but it had been in the heat of the moment and hadn't meant anything outside the sexual pleasure. It definitely hadn't elicited a reaction like that from him.

Maybe it's because I know his scent? Maybe it somehow intensifies it? Taylor's wolf had definitely liked their mixed scents. He'd even felt proud when he'd seen Kevin in his hoodie. And wearing Kevin's T-shirt had settled something in him too. Taylor hadn't thought anything of it before, besides being a little bit bashful as he'd thought it was his alpha wolf's possessiveness at play, but now he wasn't so sure. Maybe it was something else, but what?

Then it hit him as he was looking around the table at everyone. His pack. His pack that always smelled familiar and that always settled something inside him. It wasn't exactly like the thing with Kevin, but maybe it was because his wolf didn't like the fact that Kevin considered himself a lone wolf. Maybe Taylor's wolf—Taylor—had somehow started recognizing Kevin as his pack.

He took a big sip of water. Back in San Francisco it was only him and Kevin, in each other's space all the time, everything smelling of both of them. Here, it was different. Safe and known for Taylor, but completely foreign to Kevin, who had to feel like an outsider—who *smelled* like an outsider.

Yeah, that must be it, Taylor decided. He was used to the smell of *them* so much he had stopped noticing it. Only after they'd come here, after he couldn't smell it any longer, especially not after they'd both taken a shower and any effect of their clothes was gone, only then had Taylor realized what was missing. So when he'd scented Kevin, he'd gotten smell-drunk on it, especially since the neck was one of the few places the smell was the strongest. When Taylor had put his nose against Kevin's skin, he'd stopped thinking, senses overcoming any coherent thought.

"Are you okay?" Mom A asked, leaning closer to whisper in his ear. She was sitting at the head of the table, with the Beta on her left and Taylor on the right.

He nodded automatically. "Just tired after the flight."

She glanced up a little to his right. Probably at Kevin whom he hadn't exchanged a word with since they'd sat down. "Are you sure?"

No. "Yes. Just tired," he repeated. "We'll be in shape tomorrow morning, though. I promise."

She nodded. Taylor suspected he didn't convince her, but she decided to let it go and he was grateful for that.

"Good. I'm sure there will be plenty for you two to do."

Taylor chuckled. "Of course there'll be. The wedding is less than two weeks away."

As for the werewolf tradition, all the guests gathered ten days before the wedding to start the preparations. A wedding in the pack was always a group effort and it was a way to cement the bonds between the close ones, or, in the case of werewolves from different packs, a way to get to know the other side and extend the definitions of 'mine' and 'yours'.

Before his mom had a chance to say anything else, her sister and Taylor's aunt Pamela approached her and asked quietly to talk to her in urgent matter. The Alpha nodded at Taylor and left the room to have a chat without worrying about the audience.

His other mom sent him a look with raised eyebrows and a nudge of her chin, which Taylor interpreted as, "Take care of Kevin or else." He took a deep breath and turned to see Kevin absentmindedly dragging a small piece of corn around his plate.

"Are you okay?" he found himself asking. *You don't even like corn*, he thought.

"Just tired."

He didn't know if Kevin had heard his conversation with his mother or if they were equally bad at excuses. Whatever it was, it made Taylor cringe.

"We can sleep in tomorrow morning," he said. "I can show you around before we will be pulled into the preparations."

Kevin nodded. "I would love to."

'Stilted' and 'unsure' were usually the last words Taylor would describe their conversations with, but this time they were front and center. He looked around the room, hoping it would give him another topic.

Thankfully, Kevin spoke up first. "What's our part in the preparations, exactly?" he asked, glancing up at Taylor briefly.

"Sadly, for me it's whatever needs to be done. I'm usually pulled into a dozen different things and I promise myself I won't let it happen next time. But then the next time happens and it's the same. I stopped fighting it." Taylor shrugged. "But you can choose whatever you want—seats, building a stage, decorations, shopping, driving people around…"

Kevin chuckled. "And someone sold it to me as two weeks of vacation," he teased and Taylor's shoulders dropped in relief. The tension seemed to ease up between them a little.

"I didn't lie about the food, though." He smiled. "Or the view."

Kevin smiled back. "No, you didn't. I can't wait to see more of the area."

"We can explore the forest too, but it'd be much easier to do if we're shifted. You'd have to leave your camera behind."

"I will consider it." The voice was light, but Taylor didn't miss a bit of longing there. He wondered how long it had been since Kevin had gone for a run as a wolf. How long it had been since he'd done it with company.

"Okay," he said. He promised himself to take Kevin out for a wolf run more than once before they left. No werewolf should go long without one.

"Just prepare to lose any race," Kevin continued, a small smirk in the corners of his lips. "I'm really fast as a wolf."

Taylor grinned with his teeth bared. "You know how I love the challenge."

The idea of running through the forest, racing and playing with Kevin's wolf, the sudden picture of it in his mind, made him feel lighter, happier. He'd forgotten the earlier tension as he wondered what Kevin's wolf looked like. Somehow he'd never seen Kevin shifted and curiosity burned hot inside him now.

"I know," Kevin smiled, nodding. "You're on."

* * * *

Waking up beside Kevin wasn't a totally new experience for Taylor. They had fallen asleep watching TV more than once before stumbling to their respective beds in the middle of the night. But they had never slept in the same bed. Taylor had never woken up to the sight of Kevin on the pillow next to him, face soft in the morning light falling from the window, just like he had never known before how the nook of Kevin's neck smelled like, how it made him feel to scent Kevin as *his*.

Taylor rolled out of bed and sat at the edge of it. He stretched his arms above his head and stood up, glancing at the clock—eight-fifteen. His mothers would be up by now and the coffee would be ready, maybe breakfast as well. Taylor sighed. It was good to be home.

He slipped into his old jeans and even older T-shirt he pulled from his closet. After a short stop in the bathroom, he glanced one last time at the sleeping Kevin and left the room. He could hear the murmur of a conversation from the kitchen. Mom B was telling a story about, Taylor realized as he continued in that direction, the latest parent-teacher conference at her school. She worked at the inclusive primary school where kids of all species could learn, and it created some pretty interesting—or scary, or hilarious—situations she was always sharing with them, usually over breakfast or dinner.

She stopped talking when she saw him in the doorway.

"Good morning," she said with a grin, tilting her head toward the coffee maker with a mug next to it. "Fuel for you."

"I love you," Taylor said with feeling and crossed the room. On his way, he ran a hand over Mom A's arm in greeting. He was one of the few people who could touch her without express permission. As a kid he'd thought it was extremely sad that she always had to initiate contact with others, so he hugged her whenever he could, and sometimes also when he shouldn't, breaking into the room during pack talks and gripping her legs tightly. She had always smiled, lifted him onto her hip and escorted him to the door with a kiss on his forehead. She had always thanked him too.

"Did you sleep well?" Mom A asked as he took a sip of his coffee.

Taylor nodded, sitting between them at the table. "Yes. I feel more relaxed than I've been in weeks." He rolled his head around to stretch his neck. "This place is good for me."

"Of course it is. It's your home," Mom B told him, handing him a bread basket.

He smiled at her. "True."

"Is Kevin awake yet?" Mom A sat back in her seat.

"No, he's not one for waking up early when he doesn't have to." Taylor half smirked. "I don't think we'll see him before nine-thirty."

"That's fine. Was he overwhelmed by the pack last night?" His mom could switch from being a mom and an Alpha so easily Taylor sometimes didn't know who he was talking to in the given moment. He took another sip of coffee.

"It was a lot, but he handled it okay. He's not around other wolves a lot, so that might have been weird, but he hadn't said anything."

"You both looked tense at the dinner for a while," Mom A pressed like Taylor had known she would, since she hadn't gotten a satisfactory answer last night.

"We're fine. It was just nerves, I guess. He was nervous about meeting all of you and I kind of" — he waved his hand — "reacted to it." *It was plausible enough,* Taylor thought. *And not entirely untrue.*

"A lone wolf meeting a big pack whose Alpha and Beta are also his boyfriend's parents... I can see how that could make someone nervous." Mom B nodded in understanding. She had been an outsider once too. She could probably remember how it was.

"He handled himself well, though," Mom A said and offered a small smile to Taylor. "You picked good."

Taylor drank the rest of his coffee. He didn't enjoy lying to his mothers, to his whole pack. He couldn't let them fall for it too hard. "It's just the beginning. I don't know... I'm not sure anything will come out of it, so don't treat it like this is a big deal." He shrugged. "I wouldn't even have mentioned it to you if I wasn't coming here and you hadn't threatened to throw all the unmated werewolves my way if I came alone." *As much truth as possible,* he told himself.

"I'm not planning your wedding just yet," Mom A deadpanned. "I'm merely saying I like him."

"I like him too." Mom B nodded before pointing a finger at him. "And don't downplay what you two have. It's obvious you're close."

Yeah, just not that kind of close. "He's my best friend, first and foremost."

His mothers exchanged pointed glances.

"That's a good start," Mom B told him.

Taylor shook his head. Apparently they'd made too good an impression yesterday. He had to remember to be careful and not oversell the whole thing. He wanted his moms to get off his back, not to end up heartbroken after his and Kevin's inevitable falling out. And he certainly didn't want them to blame Kevin for it. Because now that Taylor recognized Kevin as his, as a member of his pack, he couldn't bear the thought of him being cast out over something like this. He had no idea if Kevin would ever consider joining the pack officially, but Taylor knew what his wolf wanted — Kevin by his side and in his pack.

Chapter Five

Kevin barely got to eat breakfast before Taylor was pulling him out of the chair and insisting on the tour around the town.

"Before we'll get sucked into the wedding craze, man," he said. "That's our best shot."

The Beta drove Kevin and Taylor to the town's center on her way to visit the bride-to-be and from there, they went everywhere on foot. Taylor showed him the usual places, the ones he'd spent most of his time at—his schools, the shop he'd worked at during the summers, the Beta's school and the pack's community center.

Then there was the sheriff's station, where they got cookies from the red-headed woman at the main desk and a minute later they were surrounded by people when what looked like the entire department came over to say hello. Lee Tomilson, the sheriff, was also, according to what Taylor had told him earlier, a high-ranking member of the pack and the only one missing at the last night's dinner.

"I'm sorry I couldn't be there." The sheriff gestured around the station. "I was on call."

"Don't worry. I'm sure we'll have time to catch up." Taylor smiled at him. "Zack told me you're doing pretty good."

"Only 'pretty good', huh?" Lee chuckled, glancing at his deputy. "I guess I know who will be on a coffee run for quite a while."

Taylor laughed. "Oops. I didn't mean to get him in trouble."

Kevin listened with one ear to the conversation, but concentrated mostly on checking out the place. It wasn't big, probably because there was not a lot of crime in a town where most of the population comprised werewolves from the same pack. The atmosphere was familiar, teasing, and it lacked that particular tension the big city precincts Kevin had been unfortunate enough to visit a few times had.

He also noticed how Taylor easily drew people in. He didn't do anything special, didn't make a spectacle out of himself. He just had this...enticing presence. The guy had loads of charisma—Kevin had known that from their very first meeting—but it seemed like it doubled the minute he'd arrived in Harrington Hills. Which was good for Taylor, obviously, but very bad for Kevin and his tight grip on the reins around his heart.

"We have a cookout with the families and friends of the sheriff's department this Saturday," he heard Tomilson say and turned back to the conversation. "You should come. Both of you," the sheriff added, with a nod toward Kevin, who nodded back in acknowledgment, but looked at Taylor for the answer.

Taylor watched him for a moment then spoke for both of them. "If nothing comes up, we'll be happy to be there. Don't think I've forgotten your wife's heavenly peach pie."

The sheriff laughed. "Very well. I will tell her you said that. Maybe she'll make some."

After talking for a while longer, everyone at the station had to get back to work, so Kevin and Taylor left them to it.

"What's next?" Kevin asked when they paused at the bottom of the steps. He snapped a few photos of the street disappearing into the horizon.

Taylor shrugged. "I say we just walk around until we get hungry."

"Fine by me."

Harrington Hills wasn't large, but it had sprawled out over the years, as new habitants arrived. According to Taylor, the newcomers were mostly werewolves coming to settle in a quiet area without territorial issues.

"The other reason is the acceptance," Taylor said as they walked down the street with the ice creams they'd gotten at the stand as a gift from the owner, another pack member.

Pretending to be the boyfriend of the town's celebrity has surprising perks, apparently, Kevin thought.

"After my moms got together, the word got out. It's not often that the same-sex couple leads the pack and does it without any serious challenge to throw them off. As the result, there's definite higher-than-average number of LGBTQ werewolves in the pack."

"Makes sense," Kevin agreed. Werewolves weren't immune to stupidity and ignorance, and there was a fair share of packs out there that refused to even have not-straight members among them. For those longing to belong, Harrington Pack seemed like a perfect place to be. Even during their trip today, Kevin noticed several same-sex couples around, holding hands, walking closely, flirting across the small tables in the diner Taylor insisted to visit to say hi to his uncle. San Francisco was one thing, but small towns Kevin had known were usually nothing like that.

"Yeah, if I didn't have a pack, I'd probably do the same thing," Taylor said, licking his knuckles as the ice cream started melting down the cone. Kevin looked away and lifted the camera to his face, snapping a photo of a random house to distract himself.

"Mm-hmm," he muttered to let Taylor know he was listening, but didn't pull the camera down. He was going to have quite a few photos to trash later on, because he wasn't concentrating on them at all and he was taking them with one hand since he was holding his ice cream in the other.

"And here is where we'll have the wedding party," Taylor said as they came to an end of the street and suddenly they were standing on the verge of a big open space of shortly cut grass. It wasn't hard to imagine even the biggest wedding party fitting here and Kevin pictured rows and rows of tables on one side and the platform and dance area on the other as Taylor told him where everything usually was. He took a photo of the empty space and told himself to snap one during the party and after to see the transformation.

"It looks great," Kevin said honestly. It definitely topped any city venue he had ever seen.

Taylor nodded before smirking. "It may not look that great to you soon enough if you end up being fooled into moving chairs and tables."

Kevin winced. "Yeah, hopefully they'll go easy on a guy from out of town. Maybe they will give me something small and insignificant."

"Don't hold your breath," Taylor told him. "We don't discriminate when it comes to hard labor."

"That explains that time you bought your red sofa and roped me into helping you." Kevin rolled his eyes.

Taylor laughed. "Hey, that's the same sofa you've been using for months, too."

"I didn't know that then, did I? And neither did you. You just 'didn't discriminate'."

"Worked, right?" Taylor flashed his teeth and Kevin had to look away again.

"Obviously."

Taylor nudged him with his elbow. "Don't sound so put upon. I know how much you love that sofa."

"More than my own, that's for sure."

"That's because yours is half your age and will fall apart soon. You should definitely get a new one."

Kevin kept looking around the empty space to avoid Taylor's eyes. He didn't want to think about his place in San Francisco right now. "Maybe."

* * * *

The tour took them longer than they'd expected, but Kevin figured that was because they hadn't taken into account all the people who'd wanted to say hi to the Alpha's Son — and there'd been a lot of them, anywhere they went. It was after four when they came back to Taylor's family house, catching a ride back with Jack. Kevin was torn between wanting to take a nap and itching to spend some time taking photos outside, but as soon as they exited the car, Taylor gently took the camera out of his hands.

"I thought we could go for a run through the forest, if you're up for it," Taylor said and his voice was...different. He usually had this commanding presence and sure voice, but now he sounded softer and almost hesitant.

"Of course," Kevin told him and he could hear that his voice was softer too, quieter.

They exchanged smiles and something uncurled in Kevin's stomach. Not desire, not exactly, although it was always there in the background when he was around Taylor. What he felt now was contentment, anticipation, childlike wonder. *I'm going to see his wolf.*

They had never shifted around each other before. There'd been no need for it and no good opportunity. Kevin knew some werewolves had this 'show me yours and I'll show you mine' policy after they got to know each other better, but he didn't do that. Taylor had never asked, either.

Now suddenly Kevin couldn't wait. They stowed his camera safely in their bedroom then headed out through the backdoor to the edge of the forest. There was a small wooden box secured low on one of the trees to store their clothes in and they undressed quickly, not looking at each other. The second the box was closed, Kevin let himself go.

He had heard that for some werewolves, the shift was painful, but he had never experienced it like that. For him it was more like stretching and loosening his muscles. It took maybe two seconds before he was looking down at his paws from two feet up. When he raised his head, he almost let out a small whine at the sight in front of him.

Taylor's wolf was...magnificent. He was black all over and only a bit larger than Kevin, but it seemed as if he were much bigger. Kevin didn't know if it was the sunlight, lighting him up from the side, or the side effect of spending the entire day watching Taylor being treated like royalty. Or maybe it was his wolf's distinct reaction to Taylor's wolf. Whatever it was, it made Kevin still and stare at him, taking in everything, from the tail pointing up, fur looking soft and thick, to the muzzle which would look deadly and intimidating, if it weren't open in a sort of a smile.

Taylor was grinning at him and Kevin couldn't not respond in kind. He grinned back.

He was pretty sure Taylor was the one who moved closer first, but he wasn't far behind. They brushed their muzzles against each other and Kevin let himself take a long, deep whiff of Taylor's scent. He lost track of how long they stood like that, nuzzling and scenting and touching. Taylor nosed under his muzzle and pushed up a little and Kevin lifted his head up to allow him more access to his neck. If wolves could purr, Kevin was fairly certain he would be doing it right now. He closed his eyes and concentrated on the feel of Taylor against him and the overwhelming smell of their mixed scents.

Kevin wanted to let out a howl. He could feel it in his trembling muscles. He was overwhelmed. The last time his wolf snuggled to another in a similar way was when he'd been a small child and his mother had still been alive. Since then, there had been barely any physical contact with other wolves in their shifted forms, and definitely no contact like this — paired with the feel of belonging, the intoxicating smell of someone Kevin could trust.

Taylor pulled back eventually. *It had to be him*, Kevin thought, since he wouldn't make himself move away first. Their noses were almost touching while their eyes met. A moment later Taylor yelped and bounced back, before he showed him his teeth in a wolfy grin and jumped between the trees.

Kevin had no choice but follow.

With every step, every jump, he felt the tension leaking out of him. He felt happier than he could remember. It felt both familiar and foreign, like something he knew as the back of his hand and like something he was just starting to discover.

The familiar part was Taylor at his side. Back in San Francisco, Kevin had thought of them as a unit, a team. They had other friends there and they hung out in a larger group from time to time, but most of the time it was just the two of them spending time together in one of their apartments. Here, it was different. Sharing Taylor with so many people felt weird and it was something Kevin would have to get used to. Taylor was being noticed, sought out. He became the center of attention wherever he went, in any group he met in town.

Kevin knew that it would be much easier for him to dismiss his feelings as jealousy of other people's attention, instead of taking it for what it truly was — the jealousy of *Taylor's* attention. He had never considered himself a possessive person, but since they'd come to Harrington Hills, he'd learned that he might have been wrong.

Or Taylor was just an exception of the rule. It wouldn't be the first time.

The new, foreign feeling Kevin was discovering now as they ran, was the sense of freedom and belonging existing side by side. For someone who was a lone wolf most of his life, freedom meant solitude and to belong was the opposite of being free. But here, right now, they were coexisting. Running through the forest with Taylor was exhilarating and Kevin felt like they could run and never stop. Everything was right in his life now — Taylor's closeness, the fresh air, the exertion of his muscles, the road ahead. His mind was empty. He felt as if they were suspended in time and place, not really getting anywhere, just moving for the hell of it.

After a while, the scenery changed a bit. Taylor led him to the river and they stopped running, walking slowly toward the water instead. Kevin watched Taylor lower his muzzle and drink before stepping in next to him. The cold water at his front paws sent a chill through his body, but also helped him to cool off. And Kevin didn't realize how thirsty he was until he took a first gulp. He almost ducked his entire head into the water, but Taylor bucked his head against his side before he could do that. When Kevin looked up, Taylor grinned at him with open jaws and tilted his head to the nice clearing to their left, where the evening sunlight managed to get through the trees, creating a perfect place to rest. Kevin nudged him back and they got out of the river and lay down on the grass on their bellies. Their sides were brushing against each other whenever they moved. It was the easiest thing in the world to lay his head down between his front legs and let out a deep sigh.

Chapter Six

Taylor wasn't kidding when he'd told Kevin that he would end up being pulled into a variety of things that needed to be done. As the Alpha's Son, designated heir to the pack, there were things he had to do on principle and the things he had to do because it felt right. Being involved in the wedding preparations of pack members fell into the latter category. It was just another way for him to take care of the pack.

That was why Taylor currently sat in the diner and glared down at his plate, waiting for the damn construction manager to pick up his damn phone. The crew was supposed to have started building the stage Friday morning and now it was past noon and still no one was here.

"Hello," the gruff voice finally came from the other side of the call.

"Hi, my name is Taylor Harrington, I'm calling on behalf of Terry Gordon and Amanda Willis—"

"Ah, yes."

'Ah, yes'? That's it? "You were supposed to be here this morning."

"Yeah, well, there's no way we'll make it on time." The guy didn't even try to sound apologetic.

Taylor gripped his fork tighter. "Obviously, since it's already well past morning."

"We can be there Tuesday."

"Tuesday? Are you kidding?"

"Something came up—"

Taylor had had enough. "You know what? Never mind. I really don't care. Consider yourself fired. And I wouldn't count on anyone from Harrington Pack ever hiring you again." Taylor ended the call and shoved his phone back into his pocket.

Great. Just great. The wedding was only a week away and they didn't have a crew to build the stage.

Taylor had no idea what they were going to do. He picked up his burger to at least eat his lunch before it got cold, but then the guy sitting beside him at the bar turned to him.

"Couldn't help but overhear," he started with a polite tilt to his head. "Is this about the construction crew? I've noticed they're not here yet."

Taylor had heard more than once from his family and from Kevin about how he ate like a pig and always talked with his mouth full, so he at least tried to control it in public. Since his mouth was filled with food, he only nodded.

"I may have a solution to your problem, if you're willing to hire a guy who's just starting out."

Taylor swallowed and turned to face the man. "We need the job done, that's it. I don't care about the experience if he can deliver." He paused. "You're the guy?"

The man was tall and had an impressive set of shoulders. He was also a werewolf and not a part of

Harrington Pack, so Taylor suspected he was either a newcomer or just visiting.

"No, no. My brother is. He lives about an hour away up north and I could give you his number. As far as I know, he shouldn't have anything booked for this week. I don't know about the materials, but—"

"That's the one thing we do have. They're just waiting for someone to use them. I would really appreciate your brother's number," Taylor said and offered a nod and a handshake. "Taylor Harrington, nice to meet you."

The guy's eyes widened for a moment before he schooled his expression. *He didn't know who I was*, Taylor realized. "Charles Dewitt, sir. Nice to meet you too. And I apologize for my behavior. I wouldn't have cut in, if I had known I'm speaking to the Alpha's Son of the Harrington Pack." He tilted his head to show his throat.

Taylor shook his head with a smile. "Don't worry about it. You offered a solution to a problem and I'm all for hearing that."

"I'm glad to be of help." Charles pulled out his phone and scrolled through his contact list. Taylor entered the number into his phone and excused himself to go outside and make a call he didn't want the guy to overhear.

"David Dewitt speaking." The voice was definitely young. The guy was probably around twenty. Taylor hoped he wasn't making a mistake.

"Hi, my name is Taylor Harrington and I got your number from your brother, Charles."

"Hi! What can I do for you?"

Taylor told him about the work that needed to be done and money they were prepared to pay. "I know this is a short notice, but—"

"Don't worry. I can make it work. I only have one coworker, but I will make my brother help out as well. It will be ready on time."

"If you'd have a problem with manpower, I'm sure we can rope more people into helping you out," Taylor assured him. Desperate times, desperate measures.

"Great. I assume you're in the Harrington Hills area?"

"In Harrington Hills, actually." Taylor gave him a specific address and contact information to himself and to Amanda and Terry.

"Okay, we'll be there tomorrow morning."

They ended the call with polite goodbyes and Taylor sighed with relief after he disconnected. He leaned against the railing for a moment, looking down the street and thinking about the next things on his to-do list. Then he remembered about his unfinished lunch and coffee that had to be cold by now. He winced, but stood up straight and went back inside. He was still hungry and maybe Chloe, the waitress who was tending the counter, would agree to reheat the food for him.

* * * *

Kevin was sitting in the kitchen with Taylor's moms when he came home for dinner. They hadn't talked much last night and this morning Taylor had left before Kevin woke up, but after yesterday's trip and their run, all the tension they'd had between them seemed to disappear. Now they exchanged looks and smiles and the only thing that was different than their usual easy interactions was Taylor running his hand over the back of Kevin's neck and Kevin leaning into the touch. It was intended for his moms' benefit, but Taylor couldn't deny that it helped relax him after a long day. He felt more grounded just from that fleeting touch.

"Hi, everyone," he said. "I'm starving."

Kevin chuckled. "Straight to the point, of course."

Taylor grinned crookedly at him. "Don't knock it. Mom B loves to feed me."

She snorted, getting up. "Of course I do," she said, voice teasing, and he narrowed his eyes as he cleaned his hands at the kitchen sink.

"You do," he insisted.

She raised her eyebrows. "Do you want your lasagna or not?"

He closed his eyes. "Mmm, you're the best."

"Hey," Mom A protested, looking up from where she was saying something to Kevin.

Taylor raised his hands. "It's still a tie. Don't worry, Mom."

"It better be," she warned him before turning back to Kevin. The traitor was trying to hide a smile.

"Don't laugh." Taylor pointed a finger at him. "Or you won't get the lasagna."

"He will." Mom B put the dish into the oven. "He's earned it."

Taylor shook his head. "I've earned it too!"

"Sit down and wait, then."

It was only the four of them tonight, since the twins were out with their friends, and apparently it meant low-key dinner around the kitchen table. Taylor was both glad and anxious that Kevin fitted so well, that his moms didn't care about eating like this instead of in the dining room where they always ate when they had guests. But he told himself not to worry about something he couldn't change—coming clean was not an option at this point, his family would never let him live this down and Kevin would be put in a really uncomfortable spot—and instead concentrate on enjoying their time here. He smiled softly at Kevin as he sat down on the opposite side of the table, and Kevin nodded, smiling back. *It was fine*, he seemed to be saying. *Relax*.

"So what did you do today? How are the preparations going?" Mom A asked Taylor. "I've heard the guys who were supposed to build the platform didn't show."

"Yeah, I called and told their boss what I think about that, but it's taken care of." He told them the story of the accidental meeting and the spontaneous hire. Then he looked at Kevin. "I will go check them out tomorrow morning and if everything goes well, I will be back around noon so we'll have some time before the sheriff's department's party. You wanted to take photos around the house—"

"He already did," Mom B said, grinning at Kevin. "I showed him everything then left him to it, because I didn't want to drag behind him."

"You wouldn't," Kevin told her. "I just know it's boring for others when I concentrate on nothing but the camera. Taylor here surely tells me a lot about it."

"Once!" Taylor protested. "I did it once." A few months ago he'd dropped by Kevin's place as Kevin had been getting ready to go for a walk, and he'd ended up tagging along. If Taylor had known Kevin would spend three hours taking photos and not saying much, he might have stayed home.

"You did it once because I had never taken you anywhere else when I was planning on just taking photos." Kevin rolled his eyes. "But you tease me about my cameras all the time."

"Taylor isn't used to playing second fiddle to anyone or anything," Mom B said, but she smiled softly at him to soften the blow.

"Hey, that's not true." He frowned.

"You're the Alpha's Son, Taylor," Mom A told him with a shrug. "You'll be leading the pack one day. The whole point is not to be the second fiddle."

"Not the *whole* point, I hope." Mom B raised her eyebrows at her mate and Mom A nodded.

"Fine. Not the whole point. But there's nothing wrong with it."

Kevin sent him a look and Taylor bit down on a laugh. So fine, maybe he enjoyed being a focus of someone's attention, but who didn't? And yes, he made an idiot out of himself when he'd huffed and kept asking Kevin if he was done already, but that was only once. And it was only because he'd been expecting the usual—that Kevin would be there with him, focused on Taylor or whatever they were doing. Not ignoring him.

Second fiddle was fine sometimes—he still wasn't at the top of the pack, after all—but he didn't do well with being ignored.

"He even took a few photos of your mother and me."

Taylor blinked, obviously missing a part of the conversation. "Wait, what?"

Mom B smirked. "Shocking, I know. Your mom and photos. But Kevin convinced her and just for that, he deserves the lasagna."

Kevin grinned at her and Taylor chuckled. Of course his mom would fall in love with Kevin. He was charming, if a little reserved when he didn't know somebody, and quiet, perfectly happy to fall into the background. He was a lot like her, Taylor realized.

"I was blackmailed into it," Mom A told him, but there was a shadow of a smile around her lips. "But it will still be nice to see them when they're done."

"Blackmail is such a strong word," Mom B said, playing innocent. "It was more like..."

"Persuasion?" Taylor tried to hold back a smile.

"Suggestion?" Kevin joined in. "A strong suggestion?"

"More like an idea, really," Mom B told them, prompting everyone to burst out laughing. Taylor had witnessed countless 'discussions' between his mothers. He knew how they usually went and who won them most of the time. It taught him to never get on Mom B's bad side.

His eyes met Kevin's across the table and Kevin's smile turned softer. Taylor felt accomplished after everything he'd done today to help out, but he had missed Kevin's company. He would have loved to have been the one to show him the area around the house, even if Kevin was glued to the camera the entire time. Taylor wished he'd been there when his mothers' session was being done too.

He was glad that tomorrow they would have a lot more time together.

* * * *

The cookout was big. Taylor had attended wedding parties in San Francisco that were smaller than this.

"Your pack sure knows how to party," Kevin told him as they stood together next to the car. They watched as Taylor's moms greeted the sheriff and his wife. "Today this, a week from now, the wedding..."

"We like to enjoy ourselves."

"Is it always like that?" Kevin asked, looking around.

"Week to week? No. But we have something at least once a month. Andrea, the sheriff's wife, takes care of the scheduling and stuff now, just so we don't have overlapping celebrations."

"Makes sense." Kevin shook his head. "I imagine having the Alpha choose where to go would be a recipe for a disaster."

Taylor nodded. "One time Mom decided not to go to either, because of the tension it would create. She sent me and the twins to one, and Mom B went to the other. After that, everybody seemed to understand the need to schedule in advance."

"Did you miss it?" Kevin asked suddenly. "The parties and everything?"

"A little, I guess." Taylor shrugged. "But not enough to travel back and forth all the time." It was the first wedding he'd come back for and it was only because Terry had basically grown up at their house. Terry and Jack had been joined at the hip since they were in preschool together.

Kevin brushed his hand over his torso for yet another time and cranked his neck. Suddenly Taylor's attention was focused only on the pale, almost white, expanse of Kevin's throat. In some kind of unspoken agreement, they'd decided not to repeat that scenting incident from the first night. Instead they did other things. Touching each other and hugging wasn't anything new, but Taylor definitely didn't use to brush his hand over the back of Kevin's neck and have Kevin lean into the touch. Kevin had also never presented his neck to Taylor before. He probably had no idea what that was doing to Taylor. His wolf couldn't ignore a gesture like that. He wanted to claim and mark, breathe in Kevin's scent, remind himself of that intoxicating smell he couldn't quite get out of his head.

Taylor was fine most of the time, keeping his wolf and his more insane ideas under control. But the pull toward Kevin was getting harder to ignore. *Perhaps I started to believe in my own game,* he thought. *Stupid.*

"Come on, let's go," he said out loud. "I was promised a peach pie."

"No, you weren't," Kevin pointed out. "You dropped a hint and the sheriff picked it up, but you don't know if his wife went with it."

She had. Taylor smiled in triumph at Kevin as Andrea not only told him she made the pie especially for him, but also assured him that he would get some of it to go.

"Find me before you leave, I had it put aside so it wouldn't get eaten."

"You're amazing," Taylor told her honestly. "Thank you so much, I appreciate it."

She smiled and nodded. "It's good to have you back."

He didn't correct her. The whole pack knew he was here for the wedding celebrations, but apparently it didn't stop some of them from suggesting otherwise. "It's good to be home," he said instead. It was true, after all.

Kevin's body tensed next to him for a moment, but before Taylor could ask, Kevin was back to his usual relaxed self. Soon after, they excused themselves and left Andrea and Lee to welcome other guests. Taylor steered Kevin straight to the nearest table. He was starving and he wanted to eat something substantial before he would stuff himself with the peach pie.

Zack found them just as they were about to eat. He nodded in greeting and sat down next to Taylor, straddling the seat.

"Listen, I wanted to ask…I've heard you handled the whole building the platform thing."

Taylor nodded, swallowing the piece of fried chicken. He ignored Kevin's muttering about how the chain of gossip was 'unbelievable' around here. Kevin had obviously never lived in a small town.

"You hired the new guy, right? Who is he?" Zack continued.

Taylor frowned. "Is there something wrong? I went there this morning. The guys seemed okay. The boss, David, is young, but he knows what he's doing. He had a basic plan ready and told me he already talked with Terry and Amanda." The soon-to-be-married couple seemed pleased as well, when Taylor called them.

"Nothing's wrong." Zack shrugged. "I was just curious since I hadn't seen the guy before and he looks...young. How did you find him?"

Taylor retold the story once again, watching with envy how Kevin ate in peace next to him.

"And that's all I know," he finished and ate another piece of chicken. "Don't worry, Deputy," he added with a smile. "I made sure he's legit. And I don't think his brother would encourage him to work if he wasn't of age."

Zack shrugged again. "Stranger things have happened. Thanks, though. Have fun and sorry for interrupting!"

Taylor watched him go, then went back to his plate. He stabbed his fork into a piece of potato when Kevin chuckled next to him.

"What?" Taylor asked.

"I don't think Zack cares if David is legit. My money is on whether or not he's *legal*."

"What's the— *Oh*." He got it and turned around, but Zack had already disappeared in the crowd. He turned back to Kevin. "Really?"

Kevin shrugged as he swallowed the food. "Just a guess. I didn't see the guy, though. Is he hot?"

"David?" Taylor paused. "I guess? He's buff, obviously, so he has that going for him. He's tall too. But he's too young."

"Not for Zack," Kevin pointed out.

"Okay, I feel old now."

Kevin snorted. "Sure, you're old. Never mind you're not even thirty." He nudged him with his elbow. "Be happy you're not perving on the jailbait."

"He doesn't look *that* young!"

Kevin burst out laughing then, throwing his head back a little, and Taylor lost his train of thought, because there it was again. Unmarked pale skin right in front of him.

He shoved another piece of potato into his mouth to avoid doing something stupid.

Chapter Seven

Kevin was going crazy. There was no way he was going to come out of all of this without losing his mind. Whenever Taylor was around, he was always touching Kevin, leaning into him, *sleeping right next to him*. Twice now Kevin had woken up in the middle of the night and had Taylor so close that their noses were almost brushing. *It would be so easy to lean in,* was his first thought both times, but then came the crushing realization that no, it really wouldn't be anything close to easy.

Nothing was exactly easy for Kevin around here, though. With the pack's constant need to drag Taylor into every little thing and with Taylor's apparent inability to say no even once, he and Kevin spent most of their days apart. It left Kevin with way too much time on his hands, so he ended up helping the Beta with her various little jobs regarding the wedding and the house. It was nice and he really enjoyed her company, but he inexplicably missed Taylor, even if they still spent almost every evening together. Time-wise, it wasn't much different than what they did in San

Francisco, but it felt different to Kevin. Back home, he had his own life, his own place. In Harrington Hills he felt surrounded by Taylor wherever he went—by his lingering scent or maybe by the mere fact that they were in Taylor's hometown, staying in Taylor's childhood home. Every place around here was filled with Taylor and yet most of the time Taylor was nowhere to be found. It left Kevin feeling lonely and out of place, which in turn made him angry at himself for being completely ridiculous.

The amount of attention he was getting was weird too. Kevin almost got used to Taylor being treated like royalty, but the pack's interest in *him* left him unsettled and too exposed. People's eyes seemed to follow him everywhere he went, even at the local supermarket.

"You get used to it," the Beta told Kevin, squinting in the midday sun. He was helping her haul the groceries into the truck in the supermarket's parking lot and he could feel the back of his neck burning from all the stares.

Kevin shrugged as he opened the car trunk. "I'm not so sure."

"If I got used to it, everybody can," the Beta said, putting her bags in. "I was so afraid of everything then. The mere thought of people looking at me was nerve-wracking. But with time, I stopped worrying." She tilted her head to the side. "I hardly notice it these days."

I won't get to do it, Kevin thought. *I won't get enough time.* "That would be nice," he said instead as he put the rest of the bags in. He could see how Harrington Hills was a part of Taylor, how his place in the pack fitted him like a glove, more than almost anything Kevin had ever seen him do. Meanwhile Kevin was an outsider, a visitor. Not to mention a liar.

"No one in the pack wishes you any harm," the Beta told him after they got into the truck and she put the key in the ignition. "They're just curious."

Kevin nodded, looking out of the window. "I know." *I'm not one of them after all.*

The Beta sighed. "You're doing fine. Relax." They drove in silence for a few minutes, then she glanced at him briefly before turning her gaze back to the road. "We're glad Taylor has someone who cares about him."

His sharp inhale was loud in his ears. *Shit.* He did not want to have this conversation with her. No way.

"The pack seems to love him," he said, pretending to stay on topic even if he knew she wouldn't buy it. "They're really happy to have him here."

Kevin saw in the corner of his eye she opened her mouth before snapping it shut. They drove in silence for a bit and he rubbed his ear as he stared out of the window.

"Of course they are," the Beta finally spoke, voice quiet and soft. Thankfully, she didn't say anything else.

* * * *

After over a week of preparations, the wedding was almost there and all they had left was the bachelor party on the eve of the ceremony. They went for the Last Run earlier in the day, the customary run of a wolf about to get married, and now the whole group took a break to change and get ready for the club.

Since Kevin had called dibs on the shower again today, now he was just waiting for Taylor to finish his own. Something had been brimming under his skin the entire day and he couldn't tell what it was. He looked down at his hands and let his claws out, staring at them. *Maybe it's the adrenaline from the run*, he decided, flexing his fingers. He needed to stop overthinking things. He should go to the party and have fun. It had been a while since he last went out and it could be nice to let loose a little bit.

Just as Kevin decided he would do exactly that, Taylor came out of the bathroom. He was half-naked and his hair was going in every direction, but he still seemed larger than life for maybe a second or two. The Alpha's Son. The words had never had more meaning to Kevin than in that short moment before their eyes met.

It was almost like an exact replica of their first evening here — the moment suspended in time as they stared at each other, not saying a word.

Kevin was the first one to look away. He sat up, blinking fast a few times to get rid of the mental pictures of all the places it could go from there, if it had been a fantasy, not real life. He rubbed his hand against his neck and told himself that no, it wasn't really tingling. *There won't be any scenting. Forget it.*

"I'll be ready in five," Taylor said, voice lower than usual. He grabbed the clothes he'd laid on the chair earlier and disappeared into the bathroom again.

Kevin let out a shaky breath. He could feel the prickling points on his neck where he dug his claws in, not enough to break the skin, but enough to shift his focus, to get rid of the cloud of want-and-need-and-*please* he found himself in.

He had no idea how they were going to get back from this. How *he* was going to get back from this.

* * * *

The club was nice. It had one big room filled with tables and booths, and the dance floor in another, connected room. They weren't the only ones in there, but with a gathering of twenty plus guys, they were definitely the biggest, impossible-to-miss group.

"First round is on me," Taylor announced with a grin, getting a cheer in response. He motioned Kevin to the seat. "I'll be right back," he said in a quieter voice, and Kevin nodded.

He looked around as Taylor went to order the drinks. He had known about half of the guests before the run earlier today and he still had problems with some of the new names now, but he easily picked out a few wolves he knew a little better. He and Taylor shared the table with Zack and another deputy, Cole, while Terry, the groom-to-be, sat at the next table with Jack and three other guys. Kevin watched Jack and Terry elbowing each other and laughing, and he wondered what it felt like to be best friends for so long. He didn't even still keep in touch with anyone he'd known when he was four.

"And I'm back." Taylor suddenly appeared, sitting down and immediately shifting closer to Kevin. "The waiters will be here with the drinks any second."

The first round turned into the second one, the third one, the fourth. Then it was just Taylor who kept putting another glass and another in front of him. The werewolves might have much higher tolerance for alcohol than humans, but they still could get drunk. And Kevin was definitely on the way to get there.

He was relaxed finally, though. He'd stopped caring about the consequences and the future and whatever else. Taylor was leaning against him, so he leaned back. Taylor threw an arm over the back of his seat, so Kevin put a hand on his thigh. He intended to do it for just a moment, at first, but then he just left his hand there.

But the worst—or the best, Kevin wasn't sure—part was the way Taylor apparently couldn't stop scenting him. The embrace, the way Kevin nearly sat on his lap... It didn't seem to be enough. Time and time again, Taylor's nose would brush against Kevin's cheek or ear. He kept away from Kevin's neck and Kevin fought the urge to just present it to him openly, but that was as far as their restraint went.

Then there was the dance floor. Kevin resisted dancing at the beginning, but the few drinks in made him more agreeable. Taylor dragged him out there and at first they danced as they always did when they would go out with friends—together but apart. It didn't last long, though. Right as the music changed, Taylor grabbed him by the hips and pulled him closer. Their chests were brushing against each other and Kevin put his arms around Taylor's neck. He was conscious about keeping his hips away. He knew that rutting against Taylor would be a bad, bad, terrible idea.

But damn, he smelled so good. Kevin was conditioned to respond to Taylor's scent at this point—couldn't stop it if he tried—but the way tipsy, sweaty Taylor plastered to him smelled like was a much harder challenge to Kevin's self-control than usual.

"Fuck, Kevin," Taylor murmured, lips against his ear. And Kevin didn't think. There was no decision. He just tilted his head—not much, but enough to send the message. He felt Taylor's shudder against his body, then Taylor leaned in and ran his nose alongside the line of Kevin's neck, making him swallow a moan. Kevin's heart was beating too fast, the music fading in the background and Kevin was becoming less and less aware of his surroundings. It was just him and Taylor, their bodies, their scents, mixing together into one and making him crazy. When Taylor's grip on his hips tightened and he felt the brush of Taylor's lips on his neck, he had to lean against him to keep standing. He forgot about his half-hard cock, the reason he was supposed to keep his distance. He just wanted to avoid the fall. It turned out Kevin didn't have to worry about embarrassing himself with an ill-timed erection. As they shifted and moved even closer, he could feel Taylor's hardness against his hip.

This time he couldn't stop a moan, but he tried to at least made it quieter and hide his face against Taylor's shoulder. The grip on his hips tightened even more and Taylor let out a muffled growl against the skin of his neck. For a few seconds, the sound reverberated through Kevin. He wanted Taylor to bite him, to leave a mark on his body, on his neck. He didn't care if others could see it. He wanted them to see it. He wanted to see it himself, look in the mirror and see the proof that it wasn't all fake, that it wasn't just him.

That thought—the reminder of what they were doing here in the first place—sent a completely different shiver down Kevin's spine. If not a complete fake, it was still a game they were playing. He shouldn't get his hopes up just because Taylor got an erection while scenting him after a few drinks. It just wasn't smart.

He closed his eyes and let himself have it for just a few more seconds—Taylor's body against his, his grip on Kevin's hips, his face in the nook of Kevin's neck. And right as he was about to pull back, the music faded to black. The DJ announced Terry's upcoming wedding and wished him all the best, before handing the microphone to Jack. The DJ's loud voice broke the spell better than almost anything could and it was easy now to pull away from Taylor.

They exchanged glances, but Kevin couldn't decipher Taylor's expression in the shadows.

"Back to the table?" he asked.

Taylor nodded, but didn't let him go, reaching out to clasp one of Kevin's hands in his before leading him off the dance floor and back to their table.

It was like slowly coming out of the dream and trying to figure out what was real and what wasn't. There was no freak out, no panic, no denial. Taylor sat down next to him and once again shifted closer, throwing his arm over the back of Kevin's seat.

Kevin waited for something, for Taylor to make a joke or come up with an excuse, for him to show Kevin how he wanted to play it, but nothing happened. It was exactly the same as before.

He had no idea what to do with that.

Chapter Eight

Taylor was usually a morning person, but there were times when he regretted his habit of waking up early and one of those times was the day after the bachelor party. They came home after three and it was now quarter past eight. He would have loved to sleep in. He'd *planned on* sleeping in. But with his mind already alert and going a hundred miles a minute, he knew it was a lost cause now.

He glanced at Kevin, still sleeping soundly at his side, facing Taylor. *What the hell is going on?* he asked himself as he watched his best friend and fought the urge to lean in closer. Taylor closed his eyes for a second before turning away to stare at the ceiling. He couldn't blame what happened last night at the club on the alcohol. They had been drunk quite a few times before in each other's company and it had never resulted in this. Taylor would laugh at anyone who would tell him there was even a little sexual tension between him and Kevin before they'd gotten here—before that first evening, when he'd scented Kevin and his whole body had been overcome by want. He hadn't called it that then — he didn't even let himself think it — but after last night Taylor could no longer fool himself. Whatever he'd felt that day wasn't a simple recognition of one of his own, his pack. He didn't react to anybody from the pack in that way. He didn't feel the loss when he pulled away from anybody else... Not like that. The pack had a particular scent, and Kevin wore it now as well, making Taylor's wolf very happy. But Kevin's scent was more than just that and Taylor wondered if he just had to smell his pack on top of Kevin's smell to suddenly go from best friends to, *You smell like mine. You should smell like that all the time.*

And the way Kevin reacted... Taylor got up quickly and went to the bathroom, shutting the door quietly behind him and clasping his hands on the edge of the sink. He stared at his reflection. His pupils were wide and he could feel his claws coming out. He could see them in the big mirror above the sink. He'd woken up half-hard, but now he was fully erect, his cock pushing against the front of his boxers. The flashes of Kevin tilting his head to the side and presenting him his neck, Kevin plastered to his body, Kevin's cock against his thigh, didn't help at all. Taylor took a few deep breaths and willed his claws to retract before palming his erection with one hand and biting his lower lip to stop a loud moan. *You can't. There's no way Kevin won't wake up and hear or smell it*, he told himself, but his hips buckled into the touch without his conscious input. He hunched over the counter.

He pulled himself together with a series of deep breaths for long enough to undress and start a shower. As soon as the water hit him, he pushed one fist against his mouth to muffle the sounds and he curled the other hand around his cock. He imagined Kevin standing in front of him, wet and naked, head bowed and tilted to the side. He pictured a series of marks on his skin—Taylor's marks. He'd been so close to licking and nipping at Kevin's neck last night on the dance floor. He'd been high on the scent of him—of them—heightened with sweat and heat, and it had taken all his restraint to stop himself. He'd considered asking for Kevin's permission when the DJ spoke up and broke the moment.

Taylor shuddered when he came, leaning against the shower wall. Through the daze, he quickly washed himself before Kevin woke up. Taylor didn't have any idea what to do, what to say. They hadn't talked about what had happened last night after they'd come home, just silently undressed and gone to bed. He'd had a fleeting thought of pulling Kevin closer, pulling him against his chest, but he'd fallen asleep too soon.

And this morning, when he'd woken up and looked over at sleeping Kevin, nothing had been quite so easy. Taylor pulled on the clothes he left in the bathroom last night before the club and decided to escape to the kitchen.

* * * *

The wedding ceremony was beautiful. Amanda and Terry stood in the middle of the large circle of pack members with only the Alpha right next to them. Surrounded and protected from all sides, they said the mating vows and exchanged the rings. Then they put their hands on each other's necks as a symbol of exchanging and mingling scents and listened to the Alpha reciting the official marriage seal.

Then there was the welcoming of the couple, where the newlyweds stood and received wishes and touches from every pack member attending. The idea was to touch both of them at the same time so their scents would mingle together in the pack members' eyes.

After that, the ceremony was over and people started to migrate to the other side of the field where the tables full of various foods were waiting. Taylor turned to Kevin. They had barely talked today and Taylor hated it, but he still couldn't come up with something to say — or rather, something he wanted to say — that he wasn't sure Kevin would run from.

"Shall we?" Taylor asked. He almost offered him his arm, but he knew Kevin would take it the wrong way and assume it was a gesture just for show.

"Sure," Kevin said and fell into step beside him. Taylor had seen this place many times in the recent week and a half, but today it looked especially lovely. All the decorations were up, all the seating arrangements issues solved, and all the various crisis situations handled.

Then right as they were about to pass through the flowery 'door' from the ceremony ground slash the dance floor to the seating area, they heard a shout behind them. They turned to see Kath Miller, the youngest daughter of the old Harrington family friend and the wedding's official photographer, lying on her side, with her camera next to her on the ground and her hand curled around her slightly round stomach.

"What happened?" Taylor heard Amanda asking as she knelt next to her friend while he and Kevin were running toward them. Terry ran past them in the other direction. "Is it the baby?"

"I don't know." Kath tried to sit down, but winced and lay back down. "It feels like cramps from hell."

"Terry went to get help, just lie here," Amanda said, taking her friend's hand.

"Do you need anything?" Taylor asked as he knelt next to them.

"Not to be in pain?" Kath squinted. "Sorry, I'm just —" She paused to bite down on her lower lip to stifle a groan. "Damn it."

They could only wait now and Taylor didn't do well with that. He turned to Kevin, who put a hand on his shoulder and squeezed, nodding.

Kath looked up. "The photos —"

"Don't worry about the photos," Amanda told her firmly. "We have some. It will be fine."

"And I took care of your camera," Kevin spoke up and Taylor noticed he was holding Kath's camera gently in his free hand. "It seems to be fine. Nothing looks damaged. It will be safe with Amanda, I'm sure."

Kath smiled between the winces. "Thanks. But I hate —"

"Kevin can take more photos, if you're really that worried," Taylor told her, but she didn't say anything else as Doc Willis, the pack's main physician, showed up next to her, Terry in tow.

Five minutes later, Kath was on her way to the clinic, and Taylor and Kevin stood next to the freshly married couple watching the doctor's car leave the parking lot.

"Here." Kevin handed Kath's camera to Amanda. "I hope you can give it back to her soon."

Amanda took the camera carefully. She looked at Kevin with a shy smile. "I hate to ask, but...I've heard you are a photographer and now Taylor said — Is there any way we could rope you into taking a few photos of the guests? Nothing fancy, just so we have something to remember today." She glanced at her husband and smiled, looking even more beautiful than during the ceremony.

"Of course," Kevin said with a nod, but shook his head when Amanda wanted to hand Kath's camera back. "I have my own in the car. I'll be fine. If you have something specific you want, let me know."

Amanda grinned at him and reached out to squeeze Kevin's forearm. "Whatever you think is right. And please, don't spend too much time on it. We just want a few photos and we wish you could enjoy our party as well."

Kevin smiled. "I'll see what I can do."

Taylor followed him to the car they had left in the parking lot.

"Are you angry I recommended you?" Taylor asked. It had been an impulse and he hadn't thought about it at the time, but he realized now he should have asked Kevin first.

"You could have played it better, but it's fine. I don't mind doing this as long as they don't have high expectations."

Taylor rolled his eyes. "Stop this. You know you're good."

"I'm mediocre at best," Kevin argued.

"You're an idiot."

That got him a slap on the arm, but he almost didn't notice as something occurred to him suddenly. Kevin and he, they were still *them*. Even after last night and some particular realizations on his part, they could still do what they always did, be the friends they were for over a year now.

When Kevin retrieved his camera bag from the trunk and they came back to the party, Kevin waved him toward their table.

"Go sit and take my bag," he said, pulling out the camera and some other things he pushed into the small pockets of his tux before handing Taylor the almost empty bag. "I will get started."

"Don't take too long," he told Kevin, but he was already walking away, concentrating on his camera. Taylor sighed. It wasn't such a good idea after all. He went over to the table where his whole family sat.

Mom A raised her eyebrows. "Where did you lose Kevin?"

"To the mistress," he said dramatically, lifting the camera bag to show her before hiding it under his chair. "He stepped in for Kath to take some photos of the party."

Mom B smiled. "How nice of him!" Although Taylor's whole family seemed to like Kevin, Mom B was definitely his biggest fan. Her enthusiasm made Taylor smile.

"I hope he won't spend the whole evening working," Julia said, turning toward the way Taylor had come from and looking around. "We're here to have fun."

"I will make sure he has fun," Taylor said without thinking and only Jack's snort into his plate made him pause. He rolled his eyes. "Seriously? What are you, fifteen?"

"Sometimes you all act like it," Mom A sighed.

* * * *

Taylor waited over forty minutes before he went looking for Kevin, which—he thought—was long enough, if not overdue. He was determined to drag him back to their table and make him eat something.

It turned out he didn't have to worry about Kevin being hungry. Taylor found him sitting on much too small chair around the children's table on the back end of the reception. Nodding in greetings at Elma, who was responsible for caring for the children, Taylor walked slowly toward Kevin behind his back. He put his finger on his lips for children not to spoil the surprise, but he was still made when the little girl sitting on the opposite seat from Kevin grinned and shouted, "Here he is!" Everyone at the table turned to look at him, so Taylor paused and smiled sheepishly.

"Hi. I seem to have lost someone and I thought you might know something."

Kevin snorted, looking down, but the children shouted excitedly.

"He's shorter than me and he's wearing a tuxedo tonight," Taylor continued, fighting a laugh. "He always walks with a camera in his hands. And he made me a promise he wouldn't be gone long, but it's been a looong time and he hasn't come back."

Kids were watching them, captivated, as Kevin looked up at him with a half-smile. "First of all, I haven't promised anything, you just assumed I agreed with you," he said with raised eyebrows. "Second of all, you told me not to work too long. As you can see" — he lifted half-eaten cinnamon roll —"I'm not exactly working right now."

"He was just telling us stories about you, sir!" the grinning girl who'd busted him earlier said.

"Oh really?" Taylor smirked down at Kevin. "And what were they about?"

Kevin stood up. "I will tell you on our way," he told him before addressing the kids. "Bye, guys, thanks for inviting me to your table!" He waved the hand he still had the cinnamon roll in. In the other he had his camera, of course.

"So, what kind of stories did you tell?" Taylor asked after they turned to walk back to their table.

"How you're learning to be an even stronger and more powerful Alpha heir in San Francisco." Kevin smirked at him. "I was embellishing a lot."

Taylor raised his eyebrows. "I bet you were." He looked around and saw couples on the dance floor. "If you're not hungry, I thought we could dance for a bit."

Kevin blushed and Taylor realized he was probably thinking about the last night's dance.

"It won't be like that," Taylor whispered, leaning closer. "I still want to dance with you, though." He would dance with Kevin in any way he would let him.

Their eyes met and whatever Kevin could read in his seemed to convince him.

"Okay," he said, voice raspy before he cleared his throat. "I just need to leave the camera somewhere safe."

After leaving Kevin's baby with Taylor's moms, who were in no hurry to go anywhere, they crossed the clearing onto the dance floor. The slow song Taylor didn't recognize started playing and he pulled Kevin close. With Kevin's arms around him and his face tucked into Taylor's neck, they fitted perfectly together. As the song progressed, Taylor relaxed more and more into it — into the embrace and the feel of Kevin around him.

They weren't physically as close as they had been last night in the club, but somehow it seemed more intimate to Taylor than their previous dance. They swayed softly to the song's melody and he breathed in deeply, closing his eyes. It was just the two of them then, Kevin's fingers playing with the hair at the back of his neck, Kevin's breath against his collarbone, Kevin's body under his hands. It took Taylor four songs to even consider changing their position and even then, he just tilted his head so that he could nose softly the taunt line of Kevin's neck and breathe in deeply at the place he could feel Kevin's quickened pulse.

"Taylor," Kevin whispered against his skin. "If you're playing—"

"I'm not," Taylor cut in and pulled back enough to look him in the eyes. "I'm not playing." He glanced at Kevin's lips. "I don't know what I'm doing, but I swear to the Moon, it's not a game."

"Good." Kevin pulled him closer, tilted his head and brushed his lips against Taylor's. It was soft and careful, because neither of them forgot where they were. They lingered, breathing each other's air, and it was perfect until Taylor licked Kevin's lower lip and Kevin's mouth dropped open. Taylor realized it was no longer enough. He wanted more, his wolf wanted more and from the look on Kevin's face, he wanted that too.

"Let's go back to the house," Taylor whispered against Kevin's mouth, not willing to pull back yet.

Kevin's fingers tightened his grip in Taylor's hair for a second before letting go. "Yes. Yes."

Chapter Nine

Taylor pushed Kevin into their room and closed the door with a soft kick before he led him to the bed, kissing him as they went. Kevin sat down on the edge of the bed and started to unbutton his shirt as he looked up at Taylor. *This is it*, Kevin thought. *This is finally going to happen.*

All the fantasies didn't measure up to the moment Taylor dropped to his knees in the space between Kevin's open legs.

"Let me," Taylor murmured and dragged Kevin's hands away from the buttons and put them on the bed. Then he dipped his finger into the space between Kevin's open collar and ran it down his chest slowly. He took care of the rest of the buttons and his finger finally reached the edge of Kevin's slacks, but then he backed off. He pulled the shirt off Kevin, running his hands over his naked shoulders and arms in the process. Then Taylor leaned down, kissed him right above his navel, and slowly made his way in the opposite direction his finger had gone. He sucked a mark low on Kevin's neck and Kevin had to grasp his shoulder for balance. He moaned as Taylor licked and nipped at his skin. He tilted his head to give him more access — *anything, everything* — and Taylor took it. He made another mark and another. Kevin's skin felt like it was on fire. His cock was painfully hard and he wanted to touch Taylor, to run his hands and lips over his body. He pushed back a little and Taylor backed away with a low groan.

When Kevin looked at him, at his wet, puffy lips and the glassy eyes, he pulled him into a hard kiss, nipping at Taylor's lower lip at the same time as he went to unbutton his shirt. Kevin needed to feel him, needed to taste. His mouth watered at the mere thought of what he wanted to do to Taylor and he had no idea where to start.

"Naked," he heard himself whisper. "Get naked."

It was an amazing idea. They undressed so quickly that they bumped into each other when they were pulling off their pants, and Kevin would have laughed but even that accidental touch sent shivers running right under his skin. When Taylor stood between his spread legs once again, this time naked, Kevin ran his hands over Taylor's chest and sides before grabbing his hips and pulling him closer so that he could seal his lips around the head of Taylor's cock. He moaned at the taste, closing his eyes. He pulled back to lick at the tip and over the underside of Taylor's cock and Taylor put both his hands on the sides of his neck, swearing under his breath. He didn't push Kevin, didn't pull, but the weight of Taylor's hands on his neck did something to Kevin. The marks Taylor had left earlier burned under his touch and Kevin moaned again before reaching down to grasp his own hard cock.

Taylor pushed him away then.

"Lie down," he rasped out and Kevin immediately complied.

Kevin didn't mind taking directions in bed — he never had — but there was something else in it now, too, as if he could release the mental barrier between his human side and his wolf and both of them would agree on this, on spreading on this bed under this man, under his Alpha. There was something primal, something deeper than conscious thought, and it made Kevin shudder and close to coming already.

"Shh." Taylor straddled him and ran his hands over his chest and shoulders. "Whatever you want. I will do whatever you want," he said, leaving another line of kisses on Kevin's chest before he licked the bruises he already left on Kevin's neck. "Just tell me what that is."

"You. Whatever you want," Kevin said, tilting his head back and buckling his hips, exposing himself in every way he knew how. He just wanted Taylor.

"Nu-uh," Taylor murmured, even as he pushed back against Kevin's hips, pinning him down. "There's almost nothing I wouldn't want to do to you now. So say it."

He was lying open under Taylor, naked, hard and exposed. He thought he gave everything, but Taylor still pushed him for more and Kevin had trouble breathing as he looked up at Taylor, naked and demanding on top of him.

He could say whatever he wanted. He wanted so much and he was so close to coming that he would be happy with whatever Taylor chose. But given the choice, given how his whole body was humming with want, there was only one thing he could say.

"Fuck me."

As soon as the words were out of his mouth, Taylor covered him with his body, leaning over him, arms resting on the both sides of Kevin's head. He attacked his mouth, licking into it without hesitation, demanding submission. He swiped his tongue over Kevin's in long strokes, not giving an inch. Kevin's grip on Taylor's shoulders had to be painful right now, but Taylor didn't seem to care. He licked over Kevin's front teeth, over the gums where the wolf's teeth were hidden, and that made Kevin keen and buckle and thrash under him. He wanted Taylor in him, now, now, *now*.

"I will. Shh, I will," Taylor was saying against his lips, still above him, as Kevin trembled. Kevin realized he was mumbling out loud and he tried to stop. He took a deep breath, but the scent of them didn't help in calming him down.

"Get in me already," he managed to pant out finally.

Taylor chuckled softly. "There you go," he whispered before moving back a bit. Kevin noticed Taylor was reluctant to pull away and that helped him get his breathing back. It wasn't just him. It wasn't.

He watched Taylor get lube with half-open eyes and he sighed in satisfaction when Taylor was back on top of him. Kevin spread his legs as wide as they would go and he was awarded with a thrust of cock against cock as Taylor leaned over for another kiss before pulling back to kneel between Kevin's legs.

With one hand on Kevin's inner thigh to hold him still and probably to drive him mad at the same time, Taylor stretched him slowly. He spent the longest time circling his finger around Kevin's entrance, spreading lube and only sometimes dipping the tip of his finger in. When he finally pushed it all the way inside, he sped up, stretching Kevin in sure, long strokes of one, then two, then finally three fingers. Kevin dug his hands in the sheets and rolled his hips to push back, but Taylor just tightened his grip on Kevin's thigh and held him down.

Then he pulled his fingers out and leaned over Kevin once more. "Okay?" Taylor whispered against his mouth and Kevin would have laughed if he wasn't so close to crying.

"Yes," he whispered back. "Please, Taylor, now."

Taylor's pupils were huge as he stared down at him. Kevin's breath caught in his throat.

"I got you," Taylor said quietly before moving back to his knees. He took his hand from Kevin's thigh only to hook that leg over his arm. Then he entered Kevin in one slow push and didn't stop until Kevin could feel Taylor's balls against his skin. They both stilled for a moment and Kevin tried to relax while he was feeling full, so full. There was no escape, no place to hide now. Taylor filled him inside and out, and when he leaned over Kevin to kiss him and the angle shifted, Kevin keened into his mouth and shuddered. He threw his hands over Taylor's neck and pulled him closer, moaning softly at the little thrusts Taylor could make from this angle. He felt amazing. Then he dragged his nails along the back of Taylor's neck and Taylor buckled in response, making Kevin shout.

After that, everything sped up. Taylor kept thrusting back and forth against his prostate and Kevin was reduced to breathless moans, unable to do anything else than take it, revel in it. He pushed back into the rhythm and he continued running his fingers on the back of Taylor's neck, but he was swept away in wave after wave of pleasure and emotions so overwhelming that his world was reduced to just this, the two of them, right here.

Then Taylor leaned in and bit on his neck and that was it. Kevin's orgasm seemed to roll through his entire body as he came between their bodies. Taylor growled into his neck and his thrusts became harder, quicker. Kevin's body was still riding the wave of his orgasm, loose everywhere but where they were connected to each other. He felt the moment Taylor stilled and came inside him, body trembling above Kevin for a split second before falling onto him.

Usually, in Kevin's experience, there was a particular end to the afterglow, even if it wasn't abrupt. But this time, it seemed like the floating would never end, like even if the body was gradually coming back from the edge, his mind was still flying high, still amazed by what just happened. Taylor's body should definitely be a dead weight on him now, but Kevin didn't feel like that at all. He felt safe and right, and he would be happy if they could stay like that forever — their bodies connected, sharing heat, Taylor's pleasant weight on him and Kevin's fingers running through Taylor's hair as Taylor nuzzled his neck.

He had never been able to drift off right after sex, but this time, when he closed his eyes, it didn't take much time at all.

* * * *

When he opened his eyes again, Taylor sat naked next to him on the bed, cleaning him gently with a wet towel. Kevin blinked a few times, wondering if he was dreaming, but the throbbing on his neck and the soreness of his ass told him everything he needed to know.

"You awake?" Taylor asked quietly, glancing up at him from where he had been staring at his chest. His hand didn't stop brushing the towel over Kevin's skin.

"Yeah," Kevin said, reaching out to run his fingers over Taylor's arm. "Sorry I drifted."

Taylor smiled. "It's fine. I took it as a compliment."

Kevin chuckled, looking away for a moment. "Of course you did."

"Shouldn't I?"

"Shut up." Kevin nudged him with his knee as he looked back at Taylor, who seemed relaxed, smiling his easy smile, and Kevin grinned, feeling loose and happy. He stretched his body out with his hands above his head and sighed.

"You're a tease. How didn't I know that before?" Taylor asked and when Kevin raised his eyebrows at him, he threw the towel away and lay down next to Kevin on his side, head resting on his bent arm.

Kevin turned to his side as well, facing Taylor, only about an inch of the space between them. He threw his leg over Taylor's and smirked. "I don't know. Am I?" He felt bold and brave, but it wasn't just any first night with someone. They knew each other. They trusted each other. And now, when Kevin knew his attraction wasn't one-sided, he didn't see the reason to hold that back.

Taylor ran his hand from Kevin's knee up his thigh to his ass, spreading his fingers there and squeezing. "I would say so, yes."

"I don't know," Kevin said, pushing back into Taylor's hand. His ass wasn't up for a repeat performance yet, but that didn't mean they couldn't do anything. "You know what they say. It's not teasing, if you intend to deliver."

Taylor chuckled, leaning in for a kiss. "They're lying," he said, lips against lips. "I'd still call that teasing."

Kevin bit his lower lip and pulled, releasing it as his fingers curled around Taylor's soft cock. "What would you call this, then?"

Taylor answered by rolling him on his back and covering him with his body. Kevin laughed into his mouth.

Chapter Ten

This time, Taylor woke up to something vastly different than the day before. He was on his side and curled against someone. *Kevin*, his mind supplied as he nosed at the back of the neck right in front of him, and he let out a satisfied rumble and licked at the warm skin. He could smell himself all over Kevin's body and the primal, usually well-hidden part of him preened in satisfaction. *Mine*.

He was soaked in Kevin's scent as well and he inhaled deeply at the mingling scent of *them*. He felt his cock waking up, but then Kevin huffed and buried his head deeper into his pillow.

"More sleep," he mumbled, still half-asleep, and Taylor chuckled, letting him go.

"Sure, however long you want," he whispered and, after a quick kiss on the back of Kevin's neck, he rolled out of bed. Taylor was wide awake now, so he decided to take a shower and go raid the kitchen. His mothers and the twins had stayed at the wedding party longer, so they might still be asleep.

As he relaxed under the shower spray, Taylor thought about last night. Two weeks ago, he would have laughed in someone's face if they told him what would happen. But now... First the scenting, then the night at the club and finally last night — they had all seemed to lead into one another in a way that was almost...inevitable.

Taylor had no idea what to do next, where to go from here, but he didn't feel the need to have it all figured out now. Instincts had led him well until now, so he would let them guide him further. He would figure it out. *They* would figure it out.

After the shower, Taylor was shaving in front of the mirror when he noticed a small mark under his collarbone. He paused and ran his thumb over it, imagining Kevin's mouth there. *Sneaky bastard.* When he glanced up to the reflection of his face, he could see his smile mirrored back at him.

* * * *

The kitchen was indeed empty when Taylor got there, but someone had put the coffee maker on timer last night and he poured himself a cup right away. He drank it as he searched through the kitchen cabinets for something to eat. He didn't know what he wanted, so he glanced over everything before finally settling on waffles. He wasn't the best at them — that title had been held by Mom A for years now — but he still knew how to do passable ones.

As he gathered the last things he needed on the counter, he heard socked feet coming down from the stairs and a moment later, Mom A appeared in the entrance, wearing a dark green robe over her pajamas and warm black socks on her feet. She didn't like wearing shoes inside, just like Taylor. He glanced at his socked feet and smiled.

"Hey," he said, lifting his head up. "I thought you'd sleep longer."

She shrugged, going straight to the coffee maker. Taylor handed her a mug.

"I woke up and couldn't sleep anymore," she said after the first sip of the coffee. "Then I heard someone in the kitchen and thought it might be you."

Taylor gestured at the counter. "I decided to make waffles. Unless you want to…" He trailed off with a hopeful look, but his mom just shook her head.

"No way, you're on your own."

Taylor nodded. "Worth a try." He poured himself another cup of coffee and glanced at his mom as she sat down at the table. "Did you have fun last night?"

"Yes, it was a nice party and the ceremony was lovely." She raised her eyebrows at him with a smirk. "Did *you* have fun last night?"

He turned to the counter. "As a matter of fact, I did. The ceremony was lovely, indeed."

"You didn't catch a lot of the party," she said and Taylor hoped he would one day achieve her level of teasing with straight face and uninterested voice.

"I've caught enough. I liked it."

There was a small snort behind him. "I bet you did."

"*Mom.*" There were things someone's own mother shouldn't tease him about and his sex life was one of those.

She chuckled. "I'm just saying."

Taylor was glad he was facing the counter, because he could feel his face heat up. He stirred the butter faster.

"But seriously, Taylor, I'm glad to see you happy with someone." His mom wasn't teasing anymore and he could sense her eyes on his back. "I didn't know what to think when you announced you were bringing Kevin last minute, but he's obviously good for you."

"It's still new," he told her, staring into the bowl. *Newer than you think.* "Neither of us really knows what we're doing." It could be true—or it could not. He hadn't asked Kevin yet where he stood on all this.

"Come here and look me in the face for this, Taylor," his mom told him and he left everything but his coffee on the counter and sat down across from her. She leaned in on her elbows. "You told us you've known each other for a long time, right?"

"Pretty much as long as I've been in San Francisco. He's my best friend, above everything else," Taylor said, gripping his mug.

She nodded. "That's good. That's important. Because what you need right now, more than anything, is trust."

"We have that." Taylor didn't need to think about it. He trusted Kevin and he knew, even before Kevin had bent his neck for him in their bedroom upstairs, that Kevin trusted him back.

"Hold on to that, then," his mom said. "If you trust him, you can be honest with him and he can be honest with you. That's a pretty good start."

"I want this to work, but that's it. That's all I know. How can I figure out the rest, though?" *How can we do this without risking what we already have?*

She chuckled, looking down on her mug. "I wish I knew the answer to that, honey."

Taylor shrugged. "You have more experience than I do."

"And most of that was trial and error," she said with a sad smile. "With your dad, it was easier. He was my first love. We were young, happy, and free to do whatever. I was the Alpha's Daughter, but I was supposed to be years from taking on the Alpha role. We had you, but we still acted like kids most of the time." She ran her hand through her hair. She didn't talk about those days often, not anymore. There was a time Taylor had asked a lot about his dad, but it had been years ago. "We would've run into some problems, I'm sure, but we just— We didn't get to it. Then he was gone and I thought that was it. There was no way I was going to get up from this." She took a sip of her coffee. "I believed that for two years. I had you and my parents, and I concentrated on that."

She paused, but Taylor knew how the story went. His grandparents had died in the car accident, a completely stupid way for two werewolves to die, but they hadn't just gotten hit. They had been pushed off the road and their car had rolled over then caught on fire. Even werewolves couldn't come back from that. Taylor's mother had become the Alpha overnight.

"With your mom, I did it all wrong," she said after a long moment of silence. "I did almost everything wrong with her and she somehow still stayed." She shook her head. "I don't recommend doing it that way. I'm not proud of how I acted. So, I wish I could tell you the right way, but I can't."

Unsure of what to say, Taylor simply nodded. It wasn't that he had no idea that it was tough for his moms in the past. His memory from those years was fleeting at best and as a child he hadn't understood most of what was going on, but over the years he stitched some of it, figured some of it out. How it wasn't easy to be the Alpha, especially while you were mourning and later, when you tried to rebuild your life with someone else. How it wasn't easy to be the Beta, especially when you came from outside and had your own issues you didn't want to talk about. How the perfect didn't exist and the good was hard to find and even harder to maintain.

And yet, still, he had never heard it from his mom like that.

She straightened in her seat. "So what I'm saying is, tough shit. You have to figure it out on your own."

Taylor startled at the sudden change of the mood, but he nodded. "Roger that."

Soon after he got back to making waffles, Mom B came down and joined them in the kitchen. They talked about the wedding and Mom B filled him in on all the newest gossip and news. Kath was fine, but Doc Willis had kept her overnight to make sure. Zack had been shooting angry looks at anybody who'd danced with David Dewitt, who apparently was 'an absolute sweetheart'. Their own Julia was making eyes at Zack's brother, Ted, and Mom A was ready to send the full on Alpha wrath on him if he would so much as breathe in Julia's direction.

"That's not true," Mom A protested, but she didn't sound convincing in the least. "He's just too old for her, that's all."

"Jack dated a guy Ted's age last year and you didn't say anything," Mom B pointed out. "You know how she's going to take it if you protest now."

"Connor wasn't that old!"

Mom B sent her a look. "Yes, he was. You know it, I know it, and she will definitely use it."

"Well, I can show her it doesn't work with the older guys, then."

"Then you'll have Jack to worry about. He'd just stopped moping about Connor. Don't open up that wound."

Taylor shook his head. Mom A might think she didn't do well, but between the two of them, his moms had raised three kids to be pretty decent adults. They did really good in his book.

When his waffles were done, he served both his moms and on impulse, he kissed Mom A on the top of her head. He caught Mom B's raised eyebrows a moment later, but he just sent her a smile to let her know everything was fine. If Mom A wanted to tell her about their conversation, she would do that, but if not, it would stay between her and Taylor. Meanwhile, he had one more person to feed.

* * * *

Taylor stopped next to the bed with two plates full of waffles and cleared his throat. Nothing. He did it again and Kevin stirred, but it wasn't until Taylor put one knee on the bed that Kevin opened his eyes. He narrowed them immediately.

"Okay, now I'm definitely dreaming."

Taylor laughed, sitting next to Kevin with one foot tucked under his thigh. "Not a dream. If it was, it would be my mom's waffles, not mine."

"Mmm." Kevin pulled himself up to sit against the headboard and ran a hand over his face. "You made waffles?"

Taylor handed him one of the plates. "I have talents you don't know about."

He saw Kevin's nostrils flare and realized what he was probably thinking about. The wave of warmth he felt at the sight of sleepy Kevin suddenly turned hotter.

"It's good," Kevin said, chewing on the food. Then he licked his thumb.

"I'm glad." Taylor stared at Kevin's mouth and watched as Kevin licked his other fingers slowly. He could feel himself getting hard and shifted on the bed.

"I thought we could go out for a run," he told Kevin to distract himself. "See the other side of the forest."

Kevin smiled and nodded. "I'd love that."

"We can go after breakfast." Taylor smiled back and leaned in for a kiss. It was chaste at first, but then Kevin swallowed the rest of the food in his mouth and opened for Taylor's tongue. He put the plate aside without looking and brought his hands up into Taylor's hair to run his fingers through it.

"You were right," Taylor murmured, licking the corner of his mouth. "The waffles aren't half-bad."

Kevin laughed into the kiss and scratched Taylor behind his ears. They finished breakfast much later.

Chapter Eleven

If Kevin thought the last run alone with Taylor was amazing, he had no words for this one. The weather was good, with the sun shining through the trees and the comfortable shadow low on the ground, the area was beautiful with seemingly endless lines of trees everywhere around them, and the company was perfect. When they shifted at the edge of the forest this time, they nuzzled for a long while, brushing against each other on all sides and nosing and nipping at each other's necks. Then Taylor nipped at him one last time and bounced to the tree line. He turned back to see if Kevin was watching before he disappeared into the forest, leaving Kevin to follow.

From then, they would run until one of them would gently tackle the other so they would stop and nuzzle each other again. It went on for a long time, but Kevin would gladly stay like that for days, not caring about anything else but each other. This time, he didn't have to be careful, didn't have to wonder if he wasn't too obvious. Taylor showered him with as much affection as Kevin offered in return. At some point, as they were resting under a bended tree, Kevin dropped the caution to the wind and rolled onto his back right before Taylor's eyes.

The time seemed to freeze for a while and Kevin stared up into the sky, not daring to turn and look at Taylor, who was like a statue next to him. Kevin couldn't even hear him breathe and he wondered if he'd be able to hear his heartbeat if he concentrated hard enough. Then Taylor rose up on all fours and slowly, very slowly, stood over Kevin's body. This time it was Kevin who held his breath. He kept looking at the sky until Taylor nuzzled at his throat, whining quietly.

When their eyes met, Kevin let out a whine of his own. They stared at each other, unmoving, as Taylor stood over him, caging him between his legs, and Kevin lay under him, completely open. *That's it*, Kevin thought, not able to look away, *that's all I've got. That's what I can give.*

Taylor leaned in and licked his neck and muzzle in long swipes of his tongue until Kevin huffed out a bark.

He was happy. He was wanted. He belonged.

He swatted Taylor on the head with one of his paws, so he would stop licking, but Taylor just nipped him in the neck in retaliation and Kevin let it go. When Taylor was satisfied enough to move on from licking his neck and muzzle, he moved lower to sniff and brush over every part of Kevin's body. Kevin made himself lie still, tilting his head to watch as Taylor explored his body as a wolf. It wasn't exactly comfortable. In the back of his head his animal instinct was protesting, screaming of danger and being too open, but Kevin had already made the leap and he wasn't going to back down. It was too late now. He'd already offered himself.

After Taylor finished exploring and scenting, he nudged Kevin with his nose to roll onto his side and when Kevin complied, Taylor lay down right next to him, resting his head over Kevin's middle. Taylor let out a deep sigh and Kevin relaxed in response, not thinking of anything besides the two of them, right here.

* * * *

They stuck close after they'd changed and dressed, and they headed back to the house. Kevin could feel Taylor's arm brush against his every step they took and it helped him to stay present while he felt something in him tremble and shake. Logically, he knew it was most likely due to the emotional high of the run coming to an end, now that his brain came back online and all the worries came back with it. But emotionally, he just felt open and exposed in a way he had never felt before, and that scared him.

When Taylor led him straight up to their room, bypassing the kitchen where the Beta and the twins were, Kevin sighed in relief. He needed it to be just the two of them for a while longer.

Taylor's phone rang as soon as the door closed behind them and Kevin tensed as he watched him picked it up.

"Hello. Oh, hi, Sheriff, what can I do for you?" Taylor half turned away from Kevin and furrowed his eyebrows, and Kevin knew how this would go. He had seen this countless times in the last week and a half. He turned away as well and moved to stand next to the dresser where he'd left his camera earlier. He brushed the fingers over it as he listened to Taylor making plans to meet with the sheriff right away.

Kevin closed his eyes and felt the trembling growing bigger inside him. He crossed his arms over his stomach, hoping it would help, but then Taylor disconnected his call and looked at him, and Kevin didn't have to hear anything. He already knew how Taylor's Alpha face looked like.

"I have to go."

Kevin felt as his hands close into fists at his sides. The trembling stopped to a halt.

"No, you don't," he heard himself say. He might know how this was going to end, but that didn't stop him. Not now. Not after their run.

Taylor paused and looked at him with raised eyebrows. "You don't even know —"

"It's always something." Kevin turned to face him fully. *It's always something. It's never me.* "We've been here for almost two weeks and it's always something. I don't think you've managed to sit in one place for more than an hour before you're off, saving the day again."

Taylor looked at him like he'd started speaking in a foreign language. "What the hell? I'm just helping out. This is what I do."

"But it doesn't have to be *all* that you do!" Kevin argued. "You're allowed to say no!"

"I'm the Alpha's Son —"

Kevin felt his shoulders drop. He let his hands fall to his sides. "I know that."

"Well, maybe you don't actually know!" Taylor crossed his arms against his chest. It was obvious he was angry and Kevin suddenly realized they had never really fought before. "Maybe if you were actually a part of a pack, you'd understand what that means."

Oh. "Wow." Kevin felt cold all over, but he resisted the urge to hug himself again. *You've heard worse*, he told himself.

Taylor took a step closer. "Listen, I didn't mean—"

"Don't tell me that!" Kevin looked back at him, suddenly having his strength back. Whoever said anger was better than sadness was right. His wolf was ready to fight back. Kevin could feel his eyes flash for a second. "I'm actually surprised it's taken you this long to throw it in my face, since you're all about pack. Yes, I don't have a pack. Yes, I'm a lone wolf, living quite happily on my own, I may add." Kevin shrugged and let out a deep, slow exhale. "I know it may offend your pack-minded sensibilities, but some wolves decide to live like that and if they want to, that's not your business. It's not for you to judge."

"I'm not...offended!" Taylor protested and he looked like he wanted to come closer. Kevin hoped he wouldn't. "I'm not judging you, or anyone else. Don't put words in my mouth."

Kevin narrowed his eyes. "So it's just that no lone wolf can really understand what a pack is all about, is that it? I should just agree to anything, take everything as it is and not say anything, because I don't understand?" His shoulders slumped, anger draining out of him as quickly as it came. "I'm going for a walk," he said, then grabbed his camera from the dresser and headed for the door.

"Wait, stop!" Taylor protested, but Kevin was already out of the room. He ran down the stairs and out of the house. Taylor didn't follow.

* * * *

It took Kevin almost an hour to put down the camera and come back to the real world. It was his usual way of dealing with stuff—hiding behind the camera and forgetting everything but what he could see through the lenses—but it had its own expiration time. He hid until he couldn't any longer and apparently today his time was already up.

After he'd left the house earlier, he'd chosen the exact opposite way that they'd gone for their run. He'd ended up in a different part of the forest and as soon as the trees had covered the sight of Taylor's family home, Kevin had rolled his shoulders and picked up the camera. Now he was slowly making his way back and the tension in his body seemed to grow with every step.

The house looked even more beautiful to Kevin now than it had the first time he had seen it. There was just something about it, something that made him drawn to it, made him—

Made him want to never leave.

Kevin inhaled sharply, putting his free hand around his stomach. *Oh no.* He closed his eyes, but blocking the sight in front of him did nothing to reverse this feeling. It was already too late.

He moved forward on autopilot, keeping his eyes on the ground, and he sat down on the steps leading on to the porch. He didn't do this. He didn't get attached to places, especially those that weren't his.

Kevin swallowed and took a deep breath. *Forget it.* He picked the camera from his lap and turned it on to go through saved pictures. Some were from back in San Francisco, a few days before they'd left, when he had been walking through the park. There was one of a random building that had caught his attention that day, but now seemed completely uninteresting. Then there were photos from Harrington Hills. The yard, the forest, the house from the outside—dozens of shots trying to catch the beauty of the place. The Beta looking at the house before and after the Alpha showed up on the porch. *'The contrast between with and without'* had passed through Kevin's head and he'd loved it so much he'd written it down in his phone to remember. Then there were photos of the two of them together, the Alpha and the Beta. First they were a little stilted, staged, but soon his models had relaxed and the photos improved.

Kevin's stomach flipped over at the sight of them laughing as they talked, the way they were leaning against each other at the patio of their family home. He swallowed around the bile of jealousy.

It was... It was new to him, in many ways. It wasn't that Kevin didn't want a partner, his mate. He did. He'd just never thought... Never imagined it like this—with the big house, the big pack. But looking at these two women made him realize that if he wanted something with Taylor—if he wanted something *more*—this was probably it. This was what it was going to look like.

It was at that moment, looking at the innocent photos of Taylor's moms, that the realization hit him—the realization that was days in the making, something he'd probably refused to accept until now.

Taylor was never going to leave this town again. He was here to stay. He had a place here, carved for him years ago and just waiting for him to come back. And when he did, he just seemed to...slot in his place around here as if he'd never left. As if he never would again.

Kevin felt as if he'd been sucker punched. He hadn't lied to Taylor earlier. He'd felt good as a lone wolf most of his life. He wasn't unhappy. But now? Now he suddenly felt alone—not abandoned, exactly, he didn't think there was any conscious decision on Taylor's part. There had been no promises made, no choice, really. Kevin had just been left on the side, because he was always going to end up there.

He turned the camera off and put it next to him before hiding his face in his hands. *You've already gotten more than you thought you would,* he told himself. *You've gotten some of him. It could be worse.*

Kevin caught the Beta's scent right before he heard her coming and he sat up straighter. The front door behind him opened and closed, and he had to fight not to turn around. He felt vulnerable again and here he was, presenting his back to another wolf, more powerful than he was.

He didn't want to face her, but she didn't leave him with much choice as she sat down next to him.

"Beta," Kevin greeted with a nod. He should be grateful that it wasn't the Alpha who came to him, he supposed. The Beta was much easier to talk to, less intense.

"Harringtons are a lot of work," she said without preamble and Kevin turned his head to stare at her. She shrugged and looked at the driveway in front of them. "And Harrington Pack can be both the best and the worst thing that has ever happened to you."

This was not what Kevin expected at all. He stayed silent, waiting for her to continue.

"Taylor was five when I arrived in Harrington Hills, pregnant and seeking asylum. Jo was already famous for being a fair Alpha and I needed to feel safe."

'She'd been in an abusive relationship before,' Taylor had told him once. *'She doesn't talk about it.'*

"She accepted me into the pack and since I had no money, she invited me to her home — and I felt safe. Sure, there were things happening. I had the twins, Taylor was acting out, because suddenly there were three new people in his home and two of them would scream or cry day and night, and Jo was dealing with the pack's rapid expansion, but I felt safe. She never once told me to leave." She paused and Kevin watched as she rubbed the palm of left hand with her right thumb. "Then I was terrified because I didn't want to leave. She was the Alpha of the pack and I didn't want to leave."

Kevin sat there with his arms around his middle and wondered what he should say. He felt something start to tremble inside him, just like before.

"They don't get it," the Beta went on and she looked at him then. Her brown-green eyes staring into his made his heart clench. "All this — this home, this pack, all their traditions — is natural to them. They have never known different. They don't get how you can feel...overwhelmed. Insignificant."

Kevin glanced away, hoping she would ignore his shaky exhale. She'd landed two hard blows and he needed a moment.

"He's all about the pack and I-I'm not." He winced at his weak, quiet voice. "My mother died when I was four, so I was shuffled around. My father was never in the picture, I just knew I had a trust fund waiting for me when I grew up." Kevin rubbed his ear. "My mom always respected the local Alpha, but we'd existed mostly separately, hadn't been really a part of the pack, not like it's done here. Still, it was the Alpha's decision what to do with me after my mom died, since I had no family left. The Alpha just didn't really care. I lived in different places, a few months here, two years there." Kevin shrugged. "It was fine. Don't get me wrong. I grew up okay. But I'd never had...this." He made a circling motion with his hand. "I was always a lone wolf."

She nodded. "And you think Taylor doesn't get it."

"I think he thinks I don't get it," Kevin said, rubbing his ear again. "And maybe I don't. I know he tries to be his best for the pack—"

"But he should also try his best for you. The pack shouldn't always come first, not in a way Taylor sees it." The Beta sighed. "I think a part of it is him overcompensating for the fact he's been gone for so long. But another part is, I think, that he hasn't learned the balance yet."

"It's not just on him." Kevin took a deep breath. "How do I learn the balance?" He looked back at her. "How do I know when I should let him do his thing and when to stand my ground?" *How do I stop my insecurities from ruining my chance, if I even have one?*

She smiled at him. "You talk to him. You have the right to expect things from him and so does he, but you need to talk about this. Then it's just practice, again and again."

"That easy, huh?"

"It's never easy when both sides have things to prove." She shook her head. "And as I said, Harringtons are a lot of work. But if you're okay with things being less than easy, the results can be great."

Kevin ran his hand over the side of his neck where Taylor had marked him last night and he felt the rush of warmth sliding through him. He didn't want to let himself hope, but the Beta's words settled him a little and he couldn't help but wonder. He was okay with things being hard. He had never expected a fairytale. But the question was, what did Taylor want?

Chapter Twelve

It was close to nine-thirty at night by the time Taylor came home. He let out a deep sigh as he turned the engine off and sat back in his seat. He was cold and deep-bone tired, and the clothes were sticking to his skin, still damp from all the water. Those damn old pipes at The Brooklyn Bar had been bound to break for a few years now and Taylor wasn't too happy about the fact that they finally had while he was in town.

You're allowed to say no! Kevin's voice rang in his ears again, just like it had been for almost the entire time he'd been helping out in The Brooklyn Bar's basement. Their whole fight had been playing on the loop in his head and coupled with the memory of Kevin's expression after he'd accused him of not getting it because he didn't have a pack, it had put Taylor in a terrible mood. Thankfully all the people who were there with him had realized it fast enough and had left him alone.

Taylor gritted his teeth at the sloshing sound in his boots as he exited the car. He paused and leaned his forearm against the rolled-down driver's window, looking at the house. There were lights on downstairs, both in the kitchen and in the living room. His bedroom — his and Kevin's room — was dark and for a terrifying second, Taylor thought that maybe Kevin had left. Maybe he'd packed his bags and gone back to San Francisco, not caring about the stupid cover story anymore, too angry and too hurt to give a damn. Taylor wouldn't even blame him, not after what he had thrown in Kevin's face earlier.

But Kevin wasn't like that. He wouldn't do that to Taylor, even if he deserved it. *Loyal like a pack*, a voice at the back of his head told him, and Taylor felt a surge of longing like a shot through his chest. As he stared at his family home, he thought of settling down, of living here, staying here for good. He had always planned on that, always counted on it to be his future. But this time, a certain lone wolf from California was there next to him when Taylor pictured himself really coming back.

He closed his eyes. They could be happy here. They could run through the forest together, have dinners with his moms and the twins, find their place. But Taylor had no idea if Kevin was even remotely interested in putting down roots. He didn't know if he could picture himself here, away from the big city and in the middle of a big pack — almost at the top of one, to be precise. Taylor had known it was going to be his life for as long as he could remember and he had no idea how it felt from the outside. He had no idea how to convince Kevin that it wasn't so bad, that it was worth it. Everything, every inconvenience, every early morning call or yet another thing that needed to be done — everything was worth it, because there was nothing like pack.

And there was no one Taylor wanted to share his pack with more than Kevin.

The front door of the house opened and he saw Kevin half-hidden in the shadow. Taylor let go of the car in a hurry and walked toward him, water still sloshing in his boots. Kevin leaned against the railing of the patio steps with his arms crossed on his chest.

"The Beta saw you through the window," he said, his gaze fixed above Taylor's right shoulder. "I went out to check on you to avoid suspicion."

Taylor paused a few steps below Kevin and looked up at him. The wave of want and longing hit him again as he inhaled Kevin's scent. He had never groveled before, but he was ready to do almost anything to breach the gap between them. He knew he had a lot to make up for.

"I'm sorry for earlier," he said quietly. "I know you probably won't believe me, but what I said? I didn't really mean it. I don't think like that."

Kevin's eyes met his and they were bright in the dim light coming from the porch lamps. "You'd never treated me like less before."

Taylor took a step closer and reached out, but let the hand drop before he could touch Kevin. "I have never thought about you as less of anything," he told Kevin firmly. "I-I don't want you to be a lone wolf, but that has nothing to do with thinking it's something bad."

"Then what?" Kevin asked, glancing at the forest in the dark before looking back at him. "What does it mean?"

Taylor took another step up, feeling his heartbeat quicken. Tangled in all the lies they had told in the last two weeks, they needed to be honest with each other above all. *He* needed to be honest. "I think of you as pack. My pack." Another step, bringing him eye to eye with Kevin, close enough to share the air, close enough for Taylor to breathe him in. "I think of you as my mate."

Kevin's sharp inhale was loud in Taylor's ears. He held his breath, hoping that it wasn't a bad sign, that Kevin—Kevin who let Taylor scent him, who came apart in his bed, who had given himself up in his wolf form in the forest just this morning—wanted it just as much.

Taylor watched as Kevin dropped his arms, no longer keeping himself closed off. He stared at Taylor, gazing over his face and his body, as if he tried to find an answer to a question.

"You—" Kevin started and stopped, lifted one hand slowly to put it on Taylor's shoulder. The touch was light, hesitant, but it still sent warm shivers down his chilled body. Taylor reached out, clasped his fingers over Kevin's hand, and moved it to the side of his neck.

"Yes," he said quietly, not taking his gaze off of Kevin.

Kevin ran his thumb over the skin under Taylor's jaw and Taylor held his breath. "My mate," Kevin whispered and leaned in for a kiss, attacking Taylor's mouth as if he wanted to bring the point home, seal their fate. Taylor was more than happy to do it. He circled his arms around Kevin's waist and pulled him closer as they kissed. His senses were overflowing as his animal side simmered under his skin. *Mate. Pack. Mine.*

Kevin seemed to read him perfectly and as they broke the kiss, he tilted his head to the side, presenting his neck to Taylor. It had always been powerful, even since that first time when they did it for a cover, but this time... This time Taylor's every sense concentrated on that strip of exposed skin. He breathed in the stronger smell of Kevin as he leaned closer, then he ran his tongue up and down Kevin's neck. He stopped from time to time to suck at the flesh to leave a mark, the first, the second, another one and another. Kevin moaned next to his ear and Taylor couldn't remember ever being as happy or as grounded.

He didn't know how long they stayed like this, but they came out of their haze only when Mom A shouted from the inside of the house that she and Mom B were going up to their bedroom.

Kevin laughed and pulled back a little. "Do you think it's a suggestion?"

"Probably." Now when they parted, a chill rushed through Taylor, reminding him once again of his wet clothes. Even Kevin's shirt was now damp from where they were pressed together. "I have to say I like it."

Kevin fingers brushed against Taylor's chest as he let his hands drop. "Yeah."

Taylor left his soaked shoes right inside, taking his wet socks off as well. The rest of the clothes he pulled off right after they entered their room.

"Hot shower for you," Kevin told him, pushing him toward the bathroom.

"You're wet now too." Taylor ran his hand over Kevin's chest. "You should have one as well. We can share," he said and pulled Kevin with him.

Taylor moaned as the hot water hit his skin and the closeness of Kevin's wet body made the whole thing even more amazing. They touched and kissed, warming up under the spray and cleaning each other. Before they were done, Taylor's cock was hard, just like Kevin's.

"Come to bed," Taylor murmured against his lips after they exited the shower.

"Right behind you." Kevin smiled at him as he toweled off quickly and tossed it into the laundry basket.

Taylor led him out of the bathroom and pushed him toward the bed until he had Kevin where he wanted him — spread in the middle of the mattress, with Taylor hovering over him.

"I want you so much," he confessed against Kevin's collarbone as he started kissing down his body. "Mine."

"Yours." Kevin sighed and put his hands in Taylor's hair.

"I want you by my side, always." Taylor nuzzled Kevin's stomach. "You've been by my side for so long now, but it's taken me a long time to get it." He looked up at Kevin. "I love you."

Kevin pulled him up until they were face to face. "I love you too," he said before kissing Taylor long and deeply. "I want you by my side as well."

"Even here?"

The question slipped out before Taylor really thought about it and he tensed. He didn't want to bring it up now, didn't want to break the mood.

"Hey, look at me," Kevin whispered and Taylor realized he'd turned his head away. He met Kevin's gaze and got a smile in response. "Here you are. Listen, I—"

"I don't want to force you—"

"Stop it. Let me finish," Kevin told him when Taylor tried to cut him off. "I understand who you are. I understand what that means. I wouldn't try to keep you away from it."

Taylor ran his fingers over Kevin's cheek. "But earlier today…"

Kevin sighed and bit his lower lip before answering. "I overreacted. I was really…emotional after our run and I didn't know how you felt about me, and with the way I felt—feel—about you, having you constantly pulling away—"

"I wasn't pulling away from you," he argued, thumb brushing Kevin's lower lip.

"I believe you. I believe you didn't mean to," Kevin spoke against Taylor's finger. "But you were gone almost all the time and... I'm not clingy, I don't want all of your time, but I do want some of it."

You have it, Taylor wanted to say. *When you're around I can barely think about anything else now.* But he knew it wasn't about what he thought. "You will have it," he said in the end. "I'll be better."

"Good." Kevin smiled at him and ran his hands through Taylor's hair before settling them at the back of his head. "I'm glad." He brought him down for a kiss.

"Does that mean..." Taylor was almost afraid to ask, to hope, but he needed to know. He rested his forehead against Kevin's. "Would you come home with me?"

Kevin tightened his grip at the back of his neck. "Yes," he whispered. "I'll come home with you. We'll come here to stay."

Taylor suddenly started shaking and the muscles in his arms gave up, making him fall on Kevin. His eyes flashed when he fought to control his body. He was overwhelmed by all the emotions and his wolf's visceral reactions.

"Shh, hey, it's okay." Kevin's voice right in his ear brought him back. Taylor could feel Kevin's hands running up and down his back. Hands with claws.

Taylor shuddered again, but this time it was pure need. He was here, with his mate, in his home – *their* home. He had everything he could ever want.

When Taylor pulled back slightly so they could kiss, they both moaned. Taylor couldn't stop tasting and touching Kevin, finally marking him without the pretense of putting on an act. There was nothing between them anymore, no more barriers. When Kevin tilted his head back and Taylor sucked at the tendon of his neck to leave yet another mark, he could feel the quickened pulse right under his skin and the only thing in his mind was, *Mine. Mate.*

Epilogue

Three months later

Kevin got out from the bathroom naked and toweled off his hair on the way to the dresser. He rolled his eyes when he opened his upper drawer and saw Taylor's underwear mixed with his again. At the beginning he'd thought that Taylor had just kept forgetting he shared his closet space with Kevin now and that he continued to put his stuff in Kevin's drawers by accident. But after a month of living here together, he was convinced Taylor did this on purpose.

He heard Taylor's laughter among other guys' outside and he came up to the window after he put his boxers on. Tonight was the Alpha's birthday party and the whole yard was being filled with tables and chairs. Taylor and a bunch of pack members were setting up the seats and Kevin smiled, looking at the scene. A few months ago a different kind of party had brought him to this town with Taylor and here they were now. Not only together as a pair, but living together, making a life together. A month ago they'd packed all their things in San Francisco and moved to Harrington Hills for good. Kevin had had doubts at first, worried that they were rushing things, but Taylor had just looked at him with those eyes that made his knees weak and assured him they were going to be fine.

And they were. Taylor had it easier, obviously, since he had always planned to come back home, but Kevin couldn't complain, either. The more time he spent in this town, with this pack, the more he liked it. Small-town customs were still something he was getting used to, but it was a work in progress. Living in Taylor's family home, with his mothers and the twins under the same roof, was surprisingly easy to fall into. He had his space when he needed it and he had company when he wished to. But most importantly, he felt like he belonged.

Suddenly Taylor lifted his head and looked up to their window, noticing Kevin right away. He seemed to have a sixth sense when Kevin was involved, always knowing where he was. *He probably felt my eyes on him*, Kevin thought, feeling his cheeks heat. Taylor raised one of his eyebrows with a grin, then the idiot whistled loudly. That got other guys' attention and they looked up. Kevin quickly moved away, hoping he managed to escape from sight before anybody really noticed him. He completely forgot that he was only in his boxers. He wasn't a prude — far from it — but he also didn't want a bunch of pack members to see him almost naked. Kevin heard a low growl from the outside and shook his head. *Now he realizes what he's done*, Kevin thought, guessing that the guys were probably teasing Taylor. *Serves him well.*

He was glad he didn't hear what had been said, though. These guys' sense of humor could be a little...crude. Kevin just hoped they reined it in a little, for their own sake. Taylor's Alpha side seemed to take offense easily when it came to his mate.

Kevin put on his shirt and looked in the mirror. He noticed his grin and chuckled at himself. It had been three months and he still caught himself like this, grinning stupidly every time he even thought of himself as Taylor's mate. It didn't seem to be getting old.

He pulled open a drawer with his socks and found a bunch of Taylor's rolled-up pairs. He shook his head with a sigh. That *did* get old.

* * * *

The Beta was in the kitchen when Kevin came down to grab a glass of water.

"Do you need any help?" he asked, watching as she quickly transferred hot cookies from the baking tray onto the plates.

She shook her head. "You're a pretty good cook, but we both know you're terrible at baking anything."

Kevin nodded. "That's true. I meant more like taking it outside." There was barely any horizontal space left in the entire kitchen.

"The twins will take care of that," she said. "You can keep me company, though, if you want."

"Sure," he said, sitting down at the table with a smile. He liked everyone in Taylor's family, but he couldn't deny that he felt closest to the Beta. Maybe it was because they were the most alike, maybe because of the conversation they'd had back when Kevin had felt lost and alone, or maybe because she had a role in the pack that would one day be his. He didn't know. But whatever it was, they'd spent quite a lot of time together in the last month. She'd helped him settle in and adjust to living in the pack, sometimes offering advice that Taylor — born and raised in a pack his whole life — simply couldn't. The Beta also understood Kevin's worry about Taylor sacrificing all his time to the pack and Kevin was pretty sure she'd had a long talk with her oldest son about it after they'd moved here. Kevin still considered that issue a work in progress, but as long as there was progress, he was fine with it.

"I didn't exactly mean silent company, you know." The Beta's amused voice pulled Kevin out of his thoughts.

"Sorry. I was just thinking." He looked around the kitchen. "Where's our guest of honor, by the way? I don't think I've seen the Alpha today."

"The twins kidnapped her for half a day for a surprise celebration."

Kevin raised his eyebrows. "Will we see them in one piece again, do you think?"

The Beta chuckled. "Who knows? I heard whispers about a spa earlier in the week, so…"

Kevin stared at her. "A spa?"

"Julia's idea, no doubt. She probably wanted an excuse to go there herself."

"That would explain it." Kevin shook his head. He couldn't imagine the Alpha in a spa. "And Jack's probably taking pictures for the blackmail material."

The Beta laughed. "I didn't think of that. You're right. But I wouldn't put it past him to enjoy a massage."

"Who wouldn't?" Kevin would happily enjoy a massage himself. Maybe he could convince Taylor to give him one…

"Your eyes just glazed over." The Beta poked him lightly with a spatula. "You're so easy to read sometimes."

A knock on the open kitchen door saved Kevin from having to answer that.

"Good afternoon. May I come in?" Kath paused in the entrance. She had one hand on her belly and in the other she was holding a package wrapped in a baking paper. She was seven months pregnant and looked tired. "Taylor said it's better to keep food in the house before they sort out everything."

"Of course, come in," the Beta said, smiling and waving her forward. "Nice to see you. Put your cake wherever you can find room and sit down with me."

"Hi, Kath." Kevin smiled at her as well and stood up. "I think that's my cue to get out there and help them. See you both later."

"Kevin, wait. I wanted to ask—" Kath looked between him and the Beta. "Chin and I are getting married in a few months and I would love to hire you as a wedding photographer, if you're available."

"Oh." Kevin hesitated. "You know I'm not really a professional like you, right?" He'd planned to start doing small commissions, but he didn't want to be hired just because he was pack and the mate of the Alpha's Son.

She shook her head. "I've seen the photos you did for Amanda and Terry's wedding and they are gorgeous. Don't be too modest. You can say no, of course."

Kevin decided quickly. "I will do it. If you're sure you want me—"

"I'm sure," Kath said, nodding and grinning. "Thank you so much."

He smiled at her. "My pleasure."

* * * *

"Hey," Taylor said from behind him as he circled his arms around Kevin's waist and pulled him closer. The party was in full swing already, but somehow they hadn't had a chance to talk with each other in private yet.

"Hi." Kevin relaxed against Taylor's chest, tilting his head to rest it on Taylor's shoulder. "Everything's okay?"

"It is now," Taylor said, his breath warming the skin of Kevin's neck. "You owe me a dance or two. Come on."

Kevin grunted in a token protest, but let Taylor walk him over to the dance area.

"Don't make that face," Taylor teased him as he turned and pulled Kevin closer. "You know you like to dance."

Kevin draped his arms around Taylor's neck. "I don't like dancing in general," he muttered, hiding his smile in Taylor's shoulder. "I don't mind dancing with you, though." He'd never minded anything that put them in a close proximity like this.

"Such a compliment," Taylor teased. They danced for a few minutes before he said, "Ray Sullivan asked if I could check out the town zoning committee's new plans this weekend."

Kevin tried not to tense, since he'd been working on being better at this — them — too. He'd been working on being more understanding. But they had plans for this weekend. They were going to finally fix up Kevin's website, make it more professional.

"I told him I can't, but I will gladly look at them on Monday," Taylor continued, acting like he didn't notice any tension in Kevin. He'd had to, Kevin knew, but he was glad Taylor didn't comment on it.

"That's great." Kevin ran his fingers over the back of Taylor's neck in silent thanks. "Looks like you won them over." Since a great majority of the town was pack as well, Taylor's return was met with enthusiasm and open arms, but there were some people, like a few members of the zoning committee, who were curt with him, at best. Until now, apparently.

"Looks like," Taylor agreed. He pulled back enough to look at Kevin and Kevin couldn't help but answer his brilliant smile with a kiss.

"You're good at that."

BUILDING A HOME

Chapter One

Zack Harrington arrived at the sheriff's station five minutes after eight, and he got off his motorcycle in a hurry. The day of the full moon was never easy, but he hadn't ever overslept before.

And his boss hated tardiness, full moon or not.

When Zack entered the station, he noticed most of the people were already there, but luckily for him, the sheriff was nowhere to be found.

Zack's shoulders sagged in relief. He went straight to the little kitchenette situated at the far end of the department, nodding to a few people on the way. He needed the caffeine before he'd be ready to face the day. He poured himself a full mug then added three spoonfuls of sugar.

His partner, Portia, toasted him with her own coffee as he sat down at his desk opposite hers.

"Tell me you have some chocolate stashed," was her greeting, and Zack gave her a crooked smile.

"Hello to you, too."

She leaned in on her elbows, hands clasped together. "Oh come o-o-n-n."

Zack opened his top drawer and pulled out a chocolate bar. "Know my generosity," he said, handing it over, and Portia grinned at him.

"You're the best."

His crooked smiled turned into a smirk. "I know I am."

"I'll take all the help I can find to get me through today," Portia muttered, before putting the chocolate between them.

"Yeah."

His partner was human, but in Harrington Hills, where a vast majority of residents were werewolves, the full moon affected everyone. Any discussion had the potential to heat up, and any irritation could transform into a blowout. The town had a really low crime rate most of the time, but the department was always busy on the full moon.

Zack's plan for the day—just like every month—was to bury himself in piles of paperwork and not come out until it was time to go home or he had go out on a call. Overdue reports made for a great distraction, especially when he was trying to avoid thinking too much.

And there were things he didn't want to think about, even outside of the full moon frustrations—like David Dewitt, a guy who just wouldn't get out of Zack's head.

It had been almost four months since Zack had gone to check on a new construction team hired for a last-minute job and seen a guy he'd been immediately drawn to. He'd wanted to cross the rest of the distance between them and run his hands all over the guy's body, had wanted to come closer and inhale his scent, imprint it on his memory and his senses. Zack had never had a reaction like that to anyone, and it had been just his luck that the guy that caused it was much too young for him.

He'd fumbled through the introductions, then walked away as soon as he could. He'd tried to avoid David ever since.

At first he'd thought it would be easy, since the guy was from out of town and his job was a one-off. But that single job had led to another, and another, and more and more people seemed to gush over David and invite him to various pack gatherings, along with David's older brother, Charles, who had recently moved to Harrington Hills. Now, wherever Zack went, he seemed to find David, but he was yet to exchange more than a nod or a greeting with him.

After tonight, everything might change, though, because tonight both Dewitt brothers would become members of the Harrington Pack. Zack's wolf was elated, but the rest of him was...concerned. Sure, he was attracted to the guy, but David was barely twenty-two, while Zack was turning thirty in a few months—and he wasn't interested in casual sex anymore.

No, that wasn't right. *Of course* he was interested—in such a way that his body responded to David even from a distance, and he longed to pull him close and do many, *many* things to him. But a hook-up wasn't what he was after in the long run, and there was no way for anything else to happen with a guy almost a decade younger than him.

The same guy who had just walked into the station.

Zack straightened in his seat without thinking, as the faint trace of David's scent reached him. He turned his head and saw David approaching the front desk then talking with deputy Ortega. When Zack focused and filtered out all the other sounds, he could hear them. David's soft, polite tone came through clearer than Ortega's low voice, but Zack still heard enough to piece the story together.

David was gathering all the permits he needed to start working on the house he and his brother had bought, one of the houses that had burned in the big fire a year ago. It needed major reconstruction, so there was a lot of paperwork involved, apparently including something from the sheriff's department.

Zack tried not to think of how close this particular house was to his own apartment and how it was possible that they would bump into each other on the street now. He tried to squash both dread and excitement at the mere thought.

David must have sensed that someone was staring at him, because he turned in Zack's direction and their gazes met before Zack could look away. After a few seconds of nothing but white noise in Zack's head, he nodded in greeting, David nodded back, and that was it. There was no excuse to look any longer, and Zack made himself return to his report, even if he was just looking at the monitor and not really seeing anything. He was focused on David, on his goodbye to deputy Ortega, on the sound of his steps, then of the door closing behind him.

"What was that?" Portia asked, just as Zack decided he could relax.

"What was what?" He tried to sound casual, but he had a feeling he didn't fool her at all.

"Oh, please." Portia leaned forward. "Are you hot for the guy?"

"Don't come to me looking for new rumors, partner," he told her, voice teasing just enough to turn it into a joke. "You won't find them here."

She pointed her pen at him. "We'll see."

Hopefully, we won't, Zack thought, focusing on the screen. *Hopefully we won't see anything.*

* * * *

The Joining Ceremony was a big deal in the werewolf culture, something akin to a wedding. Both sides pledged allegiance to the other, and they were bound together from that day forward. There were ways to leave, too, but joining was much more common in the Harrington Pack. With a same-sex couple leading the pack for over twenty years now, it was an obvious message to unbound werewolves that Harringtons didn't abide blindly by traditional ways, and it had resulted in many new members over the years, most of them being people who'd thought they couldn't fit anywhere before they found their home in Harrington Hills.

Zack had been a kid when Aunt Jolene had become the Alpha. They had been a stable, well-established pack, with not even a territory dispute for years before the previous Alpha pair had died. The transition had gone fairly smoothly, all things considered, and word that the new Alpha was as fair and strong as her late father had spread quickly. Over the years, the Harrington Pack's reputation had only grown, and now even the most traditional packs in their part of the world could not dismiss them.

The pack's big expansion meant that Zack had witnessed dozens of Joining Ceremonies. Some he remembered well, some barely at all, but he couldn't recall any that had made him feel like this one did. His wolf had always been happy about new pack members, mostly due to the primal satisfaction of getting stronger as their numbers grew. This time he had to fight with himself not to shift too early, as the impulse to do so burned right under his skin. He let his claws slip out to relieve a little tension as he watched David and Charles in the middle of the pack circle, standing before the Alpha and the Beta of the pack. He couldn't keep his eyes off

David, even though it was Charles who recited the pledge first. When it was David's turn, Zack had to press his claws to his palms. *Get a grip*, he told himself, while his wolf was ready to howl to the moon in joy and excitement.

Then, finally, it was time for everybody to shift, and Zack could let himself go. And just like always after someone joined the pack, he could feel the new bonds snapping into place inside of him. *Pack. Belonging. Protection.*

When he lifted his head, he saw David's wolf — the light brown, almost white, fur darkening a bit near his paws. David held his head high, and he seemed ready for anything.

Zack wanted to stand by his side right this second.

Then the Alpha pair blocked his view for a moment, and Zack shook his head before looking down at his paws. *Stop it. Stop it right now.*

The final part of the joining was being scented by the pack — first by the Alpha and the Beta, then the high-ranked members of the pack, then everyone else. The brothers were standing a foot apart now as they greeted their newest pack-mates, one after the other. As a nephew of the Alpha, Zack was among the high-ranked, and before he knew it, he was greeting Charles, brushing against his side. Then he stood right in front of David.

Their eyes met, and Zack had flashes of him burrowing his nose in David's neck, of nuzzling his head, of closing his jaw lightly over David's throat. There was a whine lodged in Zack's chest that he tried to swallow back, but he ended up huffing shortly. It brought him out of his haze enough to brush his shoulder against David's and to inhale his scent. David smelled like freshly cut wooden blocks and paint that wasn't yet dry, and Zack had to walk away quickly before he did something stupid.

After he left the circle, he hid in the shadow of the trees at the forest entrance and watched the rest of the ceremony from afar. He didn't look away from David for the longest time.

Chapter Two

David hadn't cared about joining a new pack at first. He and Charlie had spent years without one and, as far as David was concerned, they would be fine like that going forward, too. But Charlie had really wanted this. And since he'd done so much for David in the past, saying yes, when Charlie had finally come to ask, was a no-brainer. David would never be able to fully pay off the debt to his brother, but he could do this.

By the time the Joining Ceremony rolled around, David was actually into the idea. After being invited to a few celebrations and getting to know the locals better, he was happy that if they were going to be part of a pack, it would be this one. Most of the people he came into contact with in Harrington Hills seemed really nice.

And by 'most of the people', David meant everyone except Zachary Harrington, one of the sheriff's deputies, whose picture could be in the dictionary under the definition of Hot and Angry.

They'd met on David's first day in the town, after he'd picked up a last-minute job for a wedding party.

David had noticed Zack as soon as the man had gotten out of the sheriff's cruiser and headed his way. The deputy was handsome and very tall, and his uniform fit nicely over what looked like the body of a seasoned football player. David spent his days working in construction, and he could only dream of shoulders like that.

The spell had broken right after the guy opened his mouth.

"You're the boss here?" he'd asked in that disbelieving tone that always made David grit his teeth. He'd managed to be civil only because it had been his first day, and the guy had worn a uniform. The fact that he'd introduced himself as Zachary *Harrington* helped as well.

They hadn't exchanged more than a hello ever since, but David still couldn't forget and move on. Any time he saw Zack now, he was torn between the impulse to walk away without looking back and a desire to confront him, to walk up to him and give him a piece of his mind about not assuming things about people.

Meanwhile, his wolf just wanted to rub his muzzle all over Zack.

When the big, black wolf walked up to him during the ceremony and he looked into those clear blue eyes, David had no doubt about who it was. They stared at each other for a long time, but then Zack looked away and let out a huff that David didn't know how to interpret. Did he have a problem with David joining the pack? Or was it something else? David wasn't a pushover, and he had pissed off a few people over the years, but, as far as he knew, he didn't usually rub people the wrong way right from the start.

He didn't usually react to others like he did to Zack, either, though, so maybe they both were just destined for a collision of some kind.

But then Zack stepped closer and brushed his shoulder against David's, and David needed to push his claws into the ground to stop himself from dropping down. He drew a deep breath, hoping to calm himself, but then Zack's scent hit him—metal and coffee and something he couldn't decipher—and it just made things worse. When Zack pulled back, David leaned slightly to the side to follow but caught himself in time. He was in a very public place and he was the center of attention. It was the worst time to act crazy like that.

The rest of the greetings went by in a blur of smells and sounds and new connections, and—aside from Zack—each one was a little easier than the last. David couldn't help being elated, because somewhere deep inside, he'd been afraid he wouldn't know what to do with all these new strings of connection, of belonging. He'd been worried that he would want to run, to escape—that he would see that attachment as something holding him back. Luckily, he'd been wrong. As the wolves moved in front of him, welcoming him and Charlie, it didn't feel like the pack members would take anything from him. Instead, they were the ones sharing, the ones inviting him to be with them. He didn't have to prove himself. He didn't have to jump through hoops to be seen, to be tolerated, to be accepted. The ceremony just solidified what the pack had already given him in recent months. *"You're one of us now,"* they seemed to be telling him. *"Welcome to the family."*

And for the first time in a very, very long time, he believed that maybe his family didn't have to end at two.

* * * *

David had forgotten what it felt like to run with a big pack under a full moon, since he hadn't done it in years. Now, bounding through the thick forest as he listened to the dozens of wolves move between the trees, he suddenly remembered how amazing it was, how different from running alone or with only Charlie at his side. He almost let out a howl of joy as the adrenaline rushed through his body.

After a while, the pack dispersed and split. Some wolves went back home, done with running for the night, while others kept going, but in smaller groups. David followed one of them on a whim, and he didn't miss that a certain black wolf joined the same group. David quickened his pace, wanting to prove himself, to show he was capable. *Watch me*, he thought, picturing Zack's gaze locked on him. *Watch me. I'm no longer a kid, and I know what I'm doing.*

The words came dangerously close to the ones he'd used numerous times to tell Charlie off for being overprotective. Maybe David was cursed with having to deal with the same shit over and over again.

An hour later, their group was on their way back to where the Joining Ceremony had taken place, when David decided to take a break for a bit and explore the forest more. He stopped at the small clearing and looked around, noticing an almost-perfect circle of trees surrounding the field of grass. There was a rock formation on one side and David decided to check it out, but before he was even half-way over to it, he caught the scent of metal and coffee, and he turned, telling himself his stomach didn't just flip in excitement.

Zack was standing at the edge of the clearing and, with his black fur, he was almost invisible against the trees behind him. David tilted his head to the side and Zack did the same. They kept staring at each other, but this time there was no one who would hurry them up, no one to see this and question it. No one but the two of them.

David exhaled sharply and, without turning his gaze, he took a step forward. Then he paused, waiting for Zack's move, and when it happened, when Zack took one hesitant step toward him, David grinned and took another step. Zack took the next one, David the one after that, and they slowly came closer and closer. There was even a hint of a smile on Zack's muzzle, and something in David trembled in anticipation. He had no idea what was going to happen when they would come close enough to touch, but whatever it was—

Suddenly there was a noise to David's left, and he caught the faint scent of peppermint gum that he knew all too well. A second later his brother appeared at the edge of the clearing, a gray wolf with white underbelly. David moved toward him immediately, since the last thing he needed was Charlie questioning him about Zack. He had to be very careful not to turn around, not to check if Zack was still there.

Charlie brushed his side against David's when they were next to each other and, although David wanted to roll his eyes, he also couldn't deny it was comforting to have his brother's scent on him again and not buried somewhere under dozens of other wolves. It eased him back to reality.

His brother glanced behind him, so David didn't fight with himself anymore and he did the same, but Zack was nowhere to be seen. David told himself he was relieved, and he almost believed that.

He didn't care about exploring anymore, so when Charlie tilted his head to his left in a silent question, David nodded and followed him back into thick forest. As they ran side by side, David wanted to laugh at how, even after joining the big pack, at the end of the day, they were once again back to just the two of them. Instead of laughing, he just jostled Charlie a bit and they spent the rest of the way mock-fighting.

He pushed whatever had happened at the clearing between him and Zack to the back of his head. He'd figure it out later.

Chapter Three

The morning after the full moon, Zack was walking down the street with Portia to get breakfast at the diner.

"I'm starving," she whined, quietly enough not to bring the attention of anyone other than him, thankfully.

"I know you are. You've told me like ten times already." He rolled his eyes. "You're not even a werewolf. I should be the one starving after the full moon." And he was. He couldn't wait to get his double serving of eggs and bacon.

"Well, maybe I'm starving because I'm drained after dealing with a bunch of werewolves who were edgy and shifty the whole day yesterday."

The diner was packed when they went in, and for a moment it looked like they would have to find another place to eat, but Portia announced she saw empty seats and rushed forward. Zack followed her, only to come face to face with David, who was sitting alone in his booth with coffee and a bunch of papers spread over the table.

Portia rattled her fingers on it, next to a sketch of some kind. "Hi. Do you mind company?"

Zack wanted to drag her away and disappear, but David looked up and his polite smile only grew when he noticed Zack.

Oh. Good, then.

"No, of course not." David shuffled his papers together quickly and put them away on the seat next to him. "Good morning, deputies."

"Good morning." Portia slid into the booth. "I'm Portia Sanchez. And this is Zack Harrington, but I guess you know each other, right?"

"We've met." David glanced at Zack with a quirked smile. "But we didn't have much time to talk."

Zack wondered if he meant last night or if he was calling Zack out on avoiding him during their other, accidental meetings. He hoped it was the former. Zack figured he could at least say hello now and try to start over, but before he even opened his mouth, Portia was already speaking.

"So you're not a member of the pack?

David glanced between her and Zack. "As a matter of fact I am, as of last night." He chuckled and shook his head. "I'm still getting used to it."

Chloe, the waitress, came around with David's pancakes and took Portia's and Zack's orders before disappearing again.

"Oh my, my brother wasn't kidding," David said, his eyebrows raised. "That's a big pile of pancakes."

"And you won't be able to stop eating when you start," Zack told him. "Perfect after-the-full-moon breakfast, if you ask me."

"You're new in town, aren't you?" Portia asked, dragging David's attention away from Zack, who tried not to be jealous—because that would be ridiculous.

"I moved in last week." David poured a little syrup on his pancakes. "But I lived just an hour up north before, and I've been around for a few months now, so I'm not that new, I guess."

Zack chuckled. "Oh no, you're still new."

"Really?" David narrowed his eyes as he tried to hold back a smile.

Zack tried not to respond to that, but damn, he wanted to bring that mischievous look out more often.

"So, when does someone stop being new around here?" David asked.

Chloe came by with their orders and Zack handed Portia her plate before digging into his scrambled eggs. He smirked. "When somebody newer arrives, of course."

David snorted. "Of course. So I could potentially be the new guy for years?"

"Potentially, yes, but I don't remember anyone holding that title for so long. Before you, it was Kevin Wallace —"

"Kevin?" David frowned. "The mate of the Alpha's Son?"

"Yeah." Zack suddenly remembered seeing Taylor and Kevin together for the first time at the airport, when he'd gone with the Beta to pick them up. His cousin had never looked happier, and that had been the first time since they'd been kids that Zack had felt truly jealous of him.

"I didn't know he was so new," David said, after swallowing another piece of a pancake.

"He came with Taylor for Amanda and Terry's wedding, so he really beat you by a day or two in terms of showing up here for the first time. He didn't really leave afterward. They only went back to San Francisco to pack their things, and he officially moved in about two months ago or so." Zack shrugged. "Before him, your brother was the new guy. Before him, someone else. It usually takes two or three months, maybe."

David only nodded, since his mouth was full of pancake, but Portia leaned in closer to him and said in a stage-whisper, "Our werewolves bring all the boys to the yard. And girls, too."

Both David and Zack choked at that, and Portia went back to her bacon with a satisfied grin.

"Good to know," David said, after he swallowed the food in his mouth. Then he looked from Zack to Portia and grinned. "I can appreciate that."

Portia sat up straighter next to Zack, but he didn't even glance in her direction. His gaze was glued to David in front of him.

"Which 'that', exactly?" she asked, and Zack's next exhale got stuck in his throat. "Male? Female? Both? Neither?"

"You don't waste time on pleasantries, do you?" David snorted.

Portia shrugged. "But I've been pleasant since I sat down, haven't I?"

"I guess you're right." David bit down on his thumb. "The answer's male."

Zack's first instinct was to pump his fist up in the air, but he contained himself and did nothing. Portia, on the other hand, nodded and sat back in her seat.

"That's what I thought," was her only comment.

David nodded back. "I'm glad I didn't disappoint."

"Oh, honey, I am disappointed, but that's okay."

Zack rolled his eyes. "You're married. Angela would kill you." He glanced at David. "And you."

"Oh please." Portia smirked. "Angela would... appreciate with me."

David burst out laughing and Zack forgot what he was going to say, because with his head thrown back, David had just presented his bare neck. Zack's nostrils flared at that and he had to tighten his grip on the fork. *Damn it.*

* * * *

They kept bumping into each other even more after that. David was at the diner when Zack dropped by to pick up the takeout lunch on Wednesday, then they met in a grocery store a block from Zack's apartment. On Thursday, Zack went on his early morning jog and while he was passing the burned-down remains of the old Tyson house, he noticed David standing at the freshly cleaned-up front yard, shuffling between the pages he was holding.

To his own surprise, Zack paused on the driveway behind him and, after a moment of hesitation, he spoke up. "Hi, there."

David spun in place and his frown morphed into a smile as he bridged the gap between them. "Hi."

"Working so early?" Zack's watch pointed to seven-twenty-eight, and he assumed most people slept in for as long as they could.

"I can't sleep when I'm excited, and I really want to get this project off the ground." David waved in the direction of the house with the hand holding all the papers. "Today and tomorrow are the final clean-up days. I have people coming to remove everything that needs to go. Most of the walls are fine, which is really good. There was a time when I thought we'd have to level everything." He paused. "You were probably asking to be polite, and I'm boring you, aren't I?"

Zack shook his head quickly. "You're not boring me. I'm glad you picked this place. It was sad to look at it like this." He used to hang out with Tyson's younger son in high school, and he remembered how nice this house had been before the fire.

David scratched at his jaw, and Zack noticed a shadow of a stubble on his face. He liked unshaven David a lot, he decided.

"To be honest, I picked this one mostly due to the price and the location. You don't have a lot of property for sale in Harrington Hills, and I didn't want to live in the middle of nowhere. I was planning on getting an apartment, but between me and my brother, this house will be cheaper in the long run than two rents. And I can show off my skills to potential clients, too." He sent Zack a quick smile that made him want to wipe it off with his mouth. "If I can turn a ruin into a beautiful home, I have proof that I know what I'm doing."

Zack nodded. It made sense. David had already done a couple of jobs around town after the word about his skills had spread, but fixing up a house would be even more impressive.

"I'm curious to see what you're going to do," Zack said, looking at the shell of the house, with its burned walls and empty windows.

"So do I." David smiled. "I have all these different ideas, but I would need about ten houses to fit them all in, so I need to narrow it down and make the decision already. My brother is no help at all, telling me he's going to be happy with anything. It's nice, but not really constructive."

"Tell him he's not allowed to complain later on," Zack advised. "My sister always says 'you pick', then tells me how much she doesn't like what I've chosen."

"Oh, yes, I know that one all too well. But, thankfully, Charlie only does it with takeout food."

Zack chuckled. "Lucky you. My sister once complained about a Christmas present I picked out for myself." He shook his head. "She told me to pick something, then she complained. That was the only one time I suggested a present to her. From that point forward, come Christmas time, I collect my socks and whatever book is currently on the bestseller shelf, and we're good for another year."

"You gotta choose your battles, right?"

Zack couldn't look away from David's grin, and it took him a while to realize how close they were standing, only a section of three-foot-high fence separating them. If someone was looking from the other side of the street, he or she would probably assume Zack and David were about to kiss.

You wish, Zack thought, and it threw him out of the seductive pull of David's natural charm. He took a step back and glanced at his watch again. Quarter to eight.

"I need to go."

David nodded, his smile dimming. "Of course. I should get back to my stuff anyway," he said, lifting the stack of papers.

Zack hesitated. He didn't really want to go, but he knew it was a good idea — a smart one.

"Are you going to be there on Saturday?" David asked as Zack was about to turn away. "At the Alpha's house?"

"Of course." He nodded. "I wouldn't miss it."

It was a customary welcoming party for the new members of the pack, and it was always hosted by the Alpha pair. Zack wouldn't miss it if it were for anyone else, either, but he could admit to himself that this was the first time he'd double-checked to make sure he wasn't going to be on shift or on call.

"Great." David gave him yet another grin and Zack found himself answering in kind. "See you there."

"Yeah." Zack took a step backward. "See you there."

He turned around and ran back home, but his quickened heartbeat had little to do with the physical exertion this time.

Chapter Four

David had just finished buttoning his shirt when there was a knock on his bedroom door.

"Hey, are you ready?"

"Yes, come in."

When he turned to his brother, he noticed Charlie had gone with a similar idea—black jeans and a button-down. These pack parties were pretty low-key, but being the guest of honor put more pressure on the wardrobe choice. David had never put so much thought into dressing himself before, that was for sure.

"We clean up nice," he told his brother.

Charlie smirked as he shook his head. "You work in construction, so basically any time you're clean, you look like you're making an extra effort."

"Ha, ha, keep that up and you'll be the one tearing down the roof on our house."

"Sure, if you want to end up without a rooftop *or* a brother."

There was that. Charlie might be a good back-up with some of the ground work, but he was never, ever, going to do anything that required climbing higher than three feet.

"Fine. You're helping with the paint job, though. Then we'll see how clean you can be."

"Yeah, sure. Come on. We don't want to be late."

David followed his brother to the car — the old pick-up truck that had once belonged to their father. David had tried to convince Charlie to buy something else now that he had a stable job and only himself to feed and dress, but Charlie refused to let that car go.

"How are you, by the way?" Charlie asked, after they had been driving a few minutes in comfortable silence. "With the pack."

"I'm good." David ran his hands over his thighs. "It's weird, to feel that connection constantly, but I'm getting used to it."

"It will fade into the background after a while." Charlie sounded as if he were joining a new pack every other month, but David didn't call him on it. Sometimes his brother put on this I-know-everything persona, and the best solution was to just wait it out. David had grown out of the need to pick a fight with him every time he got like this.

"I know. I remember."

David had been thirteen when their parents had died, and he and Charlie were the only ones left. He'd forgotten a lot about being a part of a pack, but not everything. And they'd never been a part of a pack this big. The pack awareness hadn't been as strong.

"What about you?" He glanced at his brother. Charlie was the one who'd wanted this, the one who'd had expectations.

"I'm good, too." Charlie nodded with a smile, and David realized he hadn't seen his older brother smile like that in far too long. "I feel like I can finally...settle, you know? Like it's not just a next stop before I get where I'm going."

David tried to hide his surprise by turning to the window. Charlie didn't talk about his feelings much, always trying to lead with his head, not his emotions. Even when they'd been talking about joining the Harrington Pack, Charlie had presented a long list of reasons why they *should* do it instead of why he *wanted* to do it. David had learned to read his brother pretty well and he could tell how much it mattered to him, but Charlie admitting it just now threw him for a loop.

"You picked a nice place to settle down," David finally said, offering his brother a smile.

Charlie nodded, but didn't say anything else, and David turned away once again.

* * * *

The party was big, but David expected nothing less at this point. There were rows of tables filled with various kinds of food and people were sitting around and talking, having a good time. He and Charlie were at the Alpha's family table as the special guests, and David kept sneaking glances at Zack, who was sitting too far away for them to talk.

"Are you looking at Zack or Ted?" Jack, the younger son of the Alpha pair, leaned in to ask quietly.

David startled and hoped he wasn't blushing. "What?"

"My sister has a crush on Ted, so..." Jack shrugged and glanced back at his twin, Julie, who was sitting on his other side and was currently talking to the Beta. "I'm trying to scope out her potential competition."

"I'm not looking at Ted," David said with a smile.

"Good. Zack, then?" Jack watched his cousins for a long moment and David opened his mouth to tell him to cut it out before someone noticed, but then Zack looked back at him. "Good choice. I guess Zack's better looking."

"Can you just...not?"

"Not talk at all or not mention—"

"Talking is fine," David cut in. "Just not about people who sit at this very table and may hear you."

Jack nodded. "Sure, okay. Good thing you didn't tell me not to talk, that's like...almost impossible for me."

"Good to know."

"Yeah, feel free to tell me when you've had enough, and don't feel like a lesser man for it. I haven't met a person I couldn't wear down."

David chuckled. "You're oddly proud of that."

"Dude, this is, like, my superpower." Jack grinned as he sat up straight in his chair. "A secret weapon, other than teeth and claws."

"And how many enemies did you take down with that super power?"

"I talked my way out of a bunch of tests in high school and two or three tickets for my driving. Does that count?"

"Sure. Why not?"

Jack's superpower also worked as a distraction. Before David realized it, he'd eaten half his weight in grilled meat and potatoes, and he and Jack had talked about everything from high school shenanigans to NASA's latest photos of Pluto. They were the same age and had quite a lot in common, which was nice. By the time he was stuffing himself with apple pie, he felt like he had gained a friend. And he'd glanced at Zack only twice, which he counted as a success.

"He's looking our way quite often, by the way," Jack said right into his ear after leaning in closer. "I'd say you have a shot."

David bit his lower lip and forced himself not to look in Zack's direction.

"Uh-oh, I think I just hopped onto his bad side," Jack added, and that made David turn.

Zack was already walking in the direction of the house.

"What happened?"

Jack raised his eyebrows. "My guess is, he got jealous. The guy you're interested in spends over an hour talking with the same man, and they're clearly having a good time. How would you feel?"

David's stomach turned at the mere thought.

"Exactly. I guess me whispering and you blushing was the last straw."

He should probably be happy that Zack cared enough to be jealous, but he felt disappointed instead. It was as if Zack didn't know he was interested and that was weird, since David thought he was quite obvious about it. Did Zack think he had already changed his mind?

Or did he simply not care enough to find out?

"He likes our kitchen."

"What?" David turned to Jack. "What did you say?"

"Zack likes our kitchen, so he's probably there. You should go for it."

"I can't just—"

"If he asks, tell him you came to use the toilet. It's behind the door on the left when you're going through the back, by the way. The kitchen is at the front of the house, just go straight through the hall."

David considered himself a pretty straightforward guy, but this seemed a bit too much.

"I don't want to throw myself at him."

Jack frowned. "And you think talking with him means that? Look. I obviously can't tell you what to do, but from where I'm standing, two guys—who are interested in each other—are currently having communication issues. So you can either leave it at that—with both of you sulking in your separate corners—or you can clear the air and go from there."

"That…doesn't sound so bad."

"Gee, thanks."

David got up and clapped Jack's shoulder. "I'll go check out that bathroom."

"Good luck."

He tried not to think about what he was going to say, because that would make him turn away and hide. He walked past the tables and nodded in greeting at various pack members, before going inside the house. He did go to the bathroom, and he stared in the mirror as he washed his hands.

You have nothing to lose, he told himself in his head. *And if Jack's right and Zack is interested…*

When he got out of the bathroom, he paused, listening. It was quiet down the hall. The only sounds he could hear were coming from the backyard, the lull of multiple voices as the party went on. David took a deep breath and headed to the kitchen.

It was a big room with an old wooden table at the center of it, now filled with dishes and pans and cake holders, just like the counters. There was also a small seat by the window and Zack stood right next to it, with one knee resting on the cushions, as he stared at the forest that seemed to be right outside the house.

"Hey," David said, hesitating in the doorway.

Zack turned, blinking, as if he'd gotten pulled out of deep thoughts. "Hey."

"Am I interrupting? I can always…" David drifted off when Zack shook his head.

"No, I just needed a break."

David nodded. "I know what you mean."

"Do you? You seemed to be having a good time." Zack grimaced as he finished the sentence, but David didn't know if it was aimed at him or at Zack himself.

"I was. I am." David stepped into the kitchen. "I was nervous about" — he waved in the direction of the backyard — "about this whole thing, the special treatment, the seat at the main table. Aside from you, I haven't really talked with anyone from your family before. To be perfectly honest, I was hoping they would seat me next to you."

Shit. There was absolutely zero chance David wasn't bright red right now. But when he glanced at Zack to gauge his reaction, the guy was staring at the floor between them.

"I think you're lucky you got Jack instead."

"Jack's cool. I don't think he's ever heard a topic he couldn't say anything about." David shrugged. "But I'm still sorry I didn't get to talk to you."

Zack looked up then, and David had to force himself not to look away. They stood like that, unmoving, and it reminded him of their full moon encounter at the clearing. He felt drawn to Zack again. He imagined crossing the space between them and —

A sound of a child running right outside the windows, screaming in delight, broke the moment, and David swayed in place.

"What did you want to talk about?" Zack asked, running a hand over the back of his neck.

What do you think? David wanted to tell him. How much clearer could he get?

"Anything." He shrugged. "I'd like to get to know you better. If you want, that is."

His hands were sweaty and his heart seemed to be working double-time. He couldn't read Zack at all. One minute David thought the guy hated his guts, the next they were staring at each other as if they couldn't look away. It confused him, and he didn't handle confusion well.

"You want to get to know me better," Zack repeated.

David hesitated. *But since I got this far...* "Yes."

"Why?"

David took a deep breath. "Are you really that clueless or are you fishing for compliments now?" He crossed his arms against his chest. "I all but threw myself at you. If you're not interested, that's fine. I just—"

He took a step back, but Zack moved forward. "No, wait."

David stopped.

"I'm...I'm not saying I'm not interested." Every word sounded as if Zack had to force it out. "I was honestly confused."

David couldn't stop the grin, but it seemed to relax Zack slightly, so he counted it as a win.

"That's good," he said after a moment. "Not the confusion, but the...the other part." There was a shadow of a smile on Zack's face, and David was ridiculously proud. "So, would you like to—"

Another shriek of joy resounded right outside the window and he chuckled, embarrassed. It was harder than any other time he'd asked someone out.

"Would you like to go out with me?" he finally said, rushing through it in fear of yet another interruption. "Preferably some place where there are no children?"

Zack nodded and smiled back at him. "Sure. That would be...nice."

They grinned at each other and David would gladly spend the rest of the party here, with Zack, but a moment later he heard the back door open. Their time was up.

Chapter Five

Zack was distracted for the rest of the night. He couldn't believe he'd said yes. He had trouble believing that the entire conversation in the kitchen had actually taken place, but the few smiles that David had sent his way throughout the rest of the party made a compelling argument. What the hell did he do?

"You all right?" Taylor appeared by his side and sat down on the bench next to him.

Most people were dancing or at least standing around the makeshift dance floor, and the rest were still at the tables. Zack thought he'd found a quiet place to sit back and watch from the distance, but he should've known someone would find him at some point. It was almost dark, and the string lights didn't reach the last bench he'd chosen, but no werewolf needed a light to find someone if they wanted to.

"Yeah, just resting," he finally told his cousin. "And you?"

"Lost Kevin to the mistress again." Taylor waved in the direction of the dance floor and Zack located Kevin and his camera pretty quickly.

"Are you pouting?" Zack asked, amused.

"No. Shut up. Are you brooding?"

"No. Shut up."

He and Taylor had been very close as kids, spending most of their time together. Then they'd drifted apart as they took to their teenage years differently — Zack acting out and rebelling against everything and Taylor trying so hard to fit his future Alpha role. They'd become close again in their early twenties, after Zack had stopped acting like an ass, and they continued to be good friends now, even with the year-and-a-half-long gap between, when Taylor had stayed in San Francisco.

"Since you know the reason for my not-pouting, are you going to tell me who you're not-brooding about?"

When Zack looked at Taylor, his cousin just offered him a cheeky grin.

"No way."

"Oh come on," Taylor teased, nudging him with his knee. "If I start guessing, this is just going to be very embarrassing for both of us."

"Don't do it then."

"As if I can leave any dirt on you alone."

Zack snorted at that. "Thanks a lot."

"That's what the family is for."

They sat in silence for a while, and Zack hoped that maybe this time he would really manage to get off the hook, but then Taylor leaned forward and rested his elbows on his thighs, eyes still glued to the dancers — or to his mate, most likely.

"Man, why aren't you happy about it?" he asked, all the teasing gone. "If it's the person Kevin thinks it is, I would think there are fewer problems now."

There may be less, but there's no escaping some of them, Zack thought. "How would Kevin know?"

Taylor chuckled. "Man, don't ask me. He called the David thing the minute you came asking about him the day he arrived for the first time."

Zack remembered that. He'd approached Taylor at the party at the sheriff's house to learn something about David, but he'd said maybe two sentences altogether — and Kevin just…figured it out? Zack tried to school his expression, but he must have failed at it, because Taylor just nodded.

"It is David, then."

"It's no one. There's nothing to say." The traitorous voice in his head added *Yet*.

"I'm the last person to give relationship advice," Taylor said, after a few minutes of silence, "but there's really not many reasons out there not to give it a try, at least. If it doesn't work, it doesn't work. But it may very well work, then you're an idiot if you didn't try."

"When did you know me not to be an idiot?" Zack told him, trying to steer away from the subject of David, or dating, or trying anything.

"Well, you had your moments between ages five and ten."

"Sounds about right."

They fell silent after that, and Zack was grateful Taylor let it go. He was still mulling around the fact that he'd said yes, and the fact that David had even asked him out in the first place. The last thing he wanted was to gossip about it.

He kept catching himself seeking David out in the crowd for the rest of the night.

* * * *

On Monday morning most of the garbage in front of the old house had been taken away, and it already looked different. Zack noticed David measuring the steps leading to the porch, and for a few seconds, he considered just passing by. David wasn't looking in his direction and it would be easy to just...keep running. But one of Zack's bad habits was choosing the hard way more times than he probably should.

"Hey," he said, not stopping, in case David didn't want to talk, but slowing down, in case he did.

David's big smile when he lifted his head and noticed him was an answer enough. Zack paused and watched him come up to the fence.

"Hey, you. I was hoping you might run this way again, since my other option was calling up the sheriff's department."

Zack frowned. "Something's wrong?" Maybe he'd already changed his mind and wanted to cancel. *Sorry, I'm not really interested after all. Jack seems like a much better fit for me.* Zack would be lying if he said he hadn't pictured that more than once since Saturday.

"Nothing's wrong. I just didn't get your number at the party." David shook his head. "Stupid, I know. I tried to find you on social media, but you're either not there or you're very good at hiding."

"Yeah, I'm not there."

"Nothing? Wow, you're tougher than I am. I resisted for a long time, but once I started, I'm pretty much everywhere." David shrugged. "I don't use it much, but I'm easy to find."

"Basically everyone I know lives in this county." Zack played with the hem of his running shirt. "We can easily meet whenever we want, so I thought, there's no need to be out there."

"Makes sense. I was the complete opposite. We moved a lot, so the Internet was the only way to stay in touch—or at least pretend to. But speaking of meeting whenever we want…" He pulled out his phone. "May I get your number?"

Zack dictated it to David, then had him send a text to his phone.

"Great. But now that we're here, maybe we can do it in person?" David asked. "Decide when and where to go, I mean. Are you free tonight?"

Zack shook his head. "No, I have a late shift today. I'm free tomorrow or Wednesday."

"Tomorrow, then? I should be done here by six, so I can meet you at seven — or seven-thirty?"

"Let's say seven-thirty, so you won't have to worry if you don't make it on time."

"Seven-thirty it is." David smiled. "And I know I was the one asking you out, but you know this town better. Where should we go? Ideally, a place with good food, quiet enough for a conversation and with little to no children."

Zack blinked and tried to think of a place. Since he'd spent half the weekend telling himself this was not going to happen, he hadn't thought about the details if it did.

The first three places he thought of, he tossed out on the merits of 'too likely to meet someone there'. He did not want to feed the gossip mill or at least make it too easy for everyone. He was pretty sure that wherever they went, someone would spot them and the news would spread, but maybe he could buy them a little time.

"Hey, you with me?" David asked and he was frowning, hand outstretched toward Zack, but he dropped it on the fence when Zack looked up.

"Yes, sorry. I was thinking of the best place. You probably know the most popular ones, so maybe we should try for something else? My partner and I found this little place by accident, when we were coming back from out of town. It's near the city limits, but the food is great."

"Sure, okay." David smiled.

"Great. I'm…looking forward to it."

That earned him an even bigger grin. "Me too. Text me the address, and I will see you there at seven-thirty tomorrow."

"Okay. I have to go now," Zack said, without looking away from David.

"Okay."

Neither of them moved and Zack wanted so badly to just lean in and… He took a step back and David mirrored him. They each took two more before Zack finally turned.

Tomorrow. They were having a date tomorrow and, with a bit of luck, he wouldn't mess things up too badly.

* * * *

Late at night, when the station had quieted down and everyone else had gone home, Zack replayed their conversation in his head and got an idea. He might not have social media accounts, but David did, and Zack was curious. He had nothing to do but old reports, so, of course, he went looking.

And what he found was a lot of photos, most of them recent, from the last year or two, but there were also old albums from David's high school years. The books weren't old enough for Zack's comfort. The ones from the graduation were from four years ago, for Moon's sake. He looked at David in his cap and gown, and he felt like a creep. David looked older than that now and he had bulked out a lot, thanks to his job, most likely, but the carefree grin from the photo was still there and he had the same captivating eyes.

What the hell am I doing? Zack asked himself, closing the tabs full of David's photos. *What the hell was I thinking?*

He pulled out his phone, half-convinced he needed to call off their date, when he found a new text from David, one he must have sent sometime after Zack had texted him the address of the restaurant.

Thanks! I can't wait to see you there tomorrow. :)

Zack stared at the smiley face at the end of the text, then reread it once, twice, a third time. He physically couldn't make himself cancel the dinner now. He pictured David's grin when he'd said yes, back in the kitchen at the Alpha's house, and the one from this morning when Zack had told him he was looking forward to the dinner.

He put his phone away. He was *not* going to bail.

No, he would go to the dinner tomorrow. Maybe they would both decide it wasn't going to work. Maybe they would be bored. Or maybe David would be the one to call it off, after all. If not, Zack was going to have to do it. Probably.

Maybe.

Chapter Six

At six-fifteen on Tuesday, David was ready to fire his plumbers, if only to make them leave already. When they finally finished five minutes later, he barely let them pick up their stuff before ushering them out. He was tempted to step on the gas on his way home, but the idea of being pulled over by one of Zack's coworkers kept him in check.

Charlie wasn't home and that let David off the hook. He didn't want to tell his brother about the date, if he could help it. Charlie's over-protectiveness had made him a real ass to any guy David had been interested in in the past, and now, with the age difference between David and Zack, Charlie would blow a gasket for sure. David didn't want to deal with him now. He'd cross that bridge another time.

He took a quick shower, then dressed in a hurry in the clothes he'd picked the previous night. He didn't have time to second-guess himself. He looked okay, and it had to be enough.

On his way to the restaurant, he started to get more and more nervous. It had been a long time since he'd last gone on a date, but he could already tell this one was different. David just... He just wanted it to mean something. Zack had been the first guy to make him think about a long-term relationship and, while it seemed stupid since he barely knew him, the pull toward Zack was undeniable.

The frustrating thing was that David couldn't read him at all. He didn't know what to think about the hot and cold treatment Zack had given him. Maybe they were both sending mixed signals?

David had a lot of time to worry, since the restaurant was farther away than he'd thought. He was pretty sure he would've missed the sign if he hadn't been looking for it. Hidden from the road by the rows of trees, the wooden cabin gave the certain charm of romantic excursion, at least at night. The warm light coming through the windows shone on the small parking lot, and he easily recognized Zack's bike. The two times David had seen it were...memorable. Zack in his leather jacket featured in quite a few of David's fantasies now.

He parked his car next to the bike and got out, running his hands over his shirt and slacks and trying to squash the nerves that were making his stomach curl.

They didn't calm down until he went inside and found Zack waiting for him at the table in one of the booths near the back. As soon as David sat down, the tension eased and he forgot about everything but the man in front of him. He wasn't sure if he thanked the waitress, who walked him to their table or if he reacted at all to her putting a menu in front of him. He just kept staring.

Zack rested his elbows on the edge of the table as he met David's gaze. "Hey."

"Hey," David replied and his voice was raspy, hesitant. Zack was dressed in all black and the way his shirt tugged at his shoulders and chest gave David ideas unsuited for a public place. And his own clothes seemed totally inadequate now.

"You look nice." Zack frowned when David laughed. "What?"

"Sorry. I mean, thank you. I was just thinking how you look great and I don't, so when you complimented me... You know, I laughed."

One corner of Zack's mouth turned up. "I wasn't lying."

"Neither was I." David let himself give Zack another once-over. "You do look great."

It was Zack's turn to laugh. "Okay, we both look good. Let's move on."

"As you wish," David said, picking up the menu.

The waitress came back with their beers, and they both ordered steaks with potatoes and salad and, when she left them again, David chuckled.

"We're pretty predictable."

Zack leaned back in his seat and raised his eyebrows. "I'm not ordering seafood or anything like that." He paused. "Restaurant or not, I know what I like."

David felt his cock twitch at that. He wasn't sure if Zack had intended that as double entendre, but David hoped he had. "Good to know. I'm like that myself."

They watched each other in silence until the waitress came back with the cutlery and a small bread basket, but when she left, Zack tilted his head slightly in his direction. "Tell me about yourself. I realized the other day that other than your job and the fact that you have a brother, I know next to nothing about you."

"Not one to listen to the town's gossip, are you?"

"There's not that much gossip about you, surprisingly. But everyone seems to agree that they like you."

David was ridiculously pleased to hear that. He had yet to meet a local he didn't like, but he didn't know if it was mutual. "It has to be my irresistible charm," he joked.

"It has to be, yes."

Zack looked straight at him when he said it and there was no hint of teasing, just stating the fact. David took a sip of his beer, hoping not to blush.

"I'm not sure I want to break the allure now." He was only half-joking. "The reality is much less glamorous."

Zack took a drink of his beer. "That's why the reality is ultimately better."

"Right." David ran his hands over his thighs. "Well, you know the sob story, I'm sure — parents died, older brother raised — "

"Why do you do that?" Zack interrupted with a frown.

"Do what? You said you wanted to know more about me."

"You made it into a self-deprecating joke. '*You know the sob story*', like you don't have the right to be sad about what happened."

David clasped his fingers hard under the table. "I don't want pity. And you know this part. Everybody does."

"So skip it, if you think I know it. But I'm not going to offer you pity, whether you tell me or not. No need to belittle your loss."

Before David could think of something to say, the waitress came over with their food. When she left, Zack sighed and leaned closer.

"Listen, I'm sorry if I pushed you too hard. It's absolutely your choice what you tell me and how you're going to do that."

David nodded. "It is my choice, but you were right. I do go for self-deprecating jokes about this. Seems like a habit now." A habit no one had ever called him on.

"We can start over, if you want?" Zack suggested, picking up his fork. "So, tell me about yourself."

David chuckled and unclenched his fingers. "Okay. Here we go. My parents are dead and my brother's the only family I have left. He's used to being more like a guardian than a brother, but I'm trying to train him out of that." He smirked. He couldn't stay serious the entire time. "We've moved a lot, so I went through many different schools. I worked odd jobs in construction, so when I graduated, it was an easy choice what to do."

"Do you like it?" Zack looked up at him from his plate. He seemed genuinely interested and David relaxed further.

"Yeah, I do. There are days when I absolutely don't want to get out of bed, but they don't happen all that often. And I like seeing things come together. Now I'm tackling renovating a house, we'll see how that turns out." He shook his head. "Getting all the paperwork ready was a nightmare, but I'm past that and the cleanup, so that's good. Today the plumbers finished, as well. Hopefully the worst is behind me."

"Why did you decide to start your own company?"

"To be my own boss and decide how things should be done." David shrugged. "I've got years of experience, but whenever I would join a crew, they would make me do the simplest tasks, because I was the youngest. And I'm not so full of myself that I don't mind doing what they tell me to, especially when the rest of the crew is more experienced, but often they weren't. And they didn't want to listen to any advice, because—again—I was too young to know anything." He frowned. "I got tired of that."

"Don't you get that from clients now?"

"I do, but not that often. That's another thing about having your own business. People automatically treat you differently when you're the boss." He paused, then smiled at Zack. "When they get over their surprise, that is."

Zack looked down at his half-empty plate before meeting David's gaze again. "Yeah, I'm sorry about my first reaction."

David nodded. "Apology accepted." They'd moved past this. He wasn't the type to hold a grudge.

"It's really impressive that you're your own boss already. I don't think I know anybody who started so young."

"I'm glad I did." David grinned. "And I don't have much competition around here, so hopefully I'll do fine."

Zack raised his beer to him. "Hopefully."

"Okay, now it's your turn. Tell me about yourself." David pointed his fork at him. "And I didn't hear any rumors, so it's all on you."

"That's a relief." A shadow passed over Zack's face, but it was quickly replaced by a dry smile. "I'm old news for this town, and they don't really have anything to gossip about now. They could live off me when I was a teenager, so I think I gave them enough."

David leaned forward. "Teenage rebellion?"

"Yeah." Zack winced. "Classic rebel without a cause. I was acting out against everything and everyone. Stupid, really."

"It's stupid now, because you grew up."

"No, I knew it was stupid then, too. I knew I was just making things worse, but..." He shrugged. "It seemed like I couldn't stop."

"You did, though." David had seen a lot of rebellious teenagers over the years in different schools. He hoped they all had stopped before it was too late.

"I did." Zack looked down at the table. "But it took me a while. I graduated a year later than the rest of my class, and I didn't know what to do with myself. There were people whom I hadn't pissed off too much who gave me some temp jobs, but it wasn't until I was clerking at the sheriff's station that I decided what I wanted to do." He rubbed his jaw. "Sheriff Tomilson almost fell off the chair when I told him. But when he realized I was serious, he really helped me out."

"That's great. Good for him." David smiled, picturing younger Zack in a leather jacket sitting in the sheriff's office. "And good for you, huh? Do you like it?"

"Yeah, I do. There's not a lot of crime going on around here, but we're still busy."

"And the uniform has to have its perks, too," David joked then laughed at Zack's surprised expression. "I'm sorry...I'm sorry."

"I don't think the uniform has ever helped me in that regard." Zack smirked.

"You never know. The first time I saw you, you were in a uniform and now look at us," David said, before he could stop himself.

Something flashed behind Zack's eyes and the temperature around the table went up. David could feel a wave of heat running through him. He licked his lips and when Zack dropped his gaze to watch him, David felt his cock harden in response.

"I hope the uniform wasn't the only selling point," Zack said, his voice lower than before.

"No." David shook his head. "No, it wasn't."
By now, there were too many of them to count.

Chapter Seven

When they left the restaurant, Zack inhaled the cold evening air to try to calm down the sizzling energy under his skin. They hadn't mentioned anything sexual throughout the rest of the dinner, but ever since that comment about the uniform, Zack had had to fight with himself not to drag David out of that place or drag him to the bathroom, at least. But they had managed to finish their meal and now they walked in silence to the parking lot, only to pause between David's truck and Zack's bike.

Then David pulled him closer and backed up to the side of his car. The feel of their bodies slotting together and the scent of David and his arousal made Zack hard in an instant. He pushed David against the truck, trapping him between his body and the car, then he leaned in. He grazed David's lower lip with his teeth before licking over the bite. There was nothing delicate about their kiss, and both of them gave as much as they got. David had his arms around Zack's waist and he used that to pull him even closer. There was no space between their bodies now and their mixing scents fueled Zack's desire. His wolf was satisfied in a way Zack couldn't remember being, and he wanted more.

They broke for air, then went right back to it, breathing harshly into each other's mouth but unwilling to move away. Zack rolled his hips to push their groins more tightly together, swallowing David's moan. The friction against his cock pushed Zack even closer to coming, and he tightened his grip at the back of David's neck. David dropped his head to the side, presenting the long strip of pale skin, unmarked and inviting. Zack nosed along the tendons, inhaling the scent and seeking out the pulse throbbing right underneath. He licked and nipped, trying to get deeper, trying to crawl inside and —

The door opened somewhere behind him, but he only half-registered it until someone cleared her throat. He froze with his face hidden in David's neck.

"Gentlemen, please take it someplace else. The pheromones are getting…noticeable inside."

Zack squeezed his eyes shut, pretending it wasn't happening, but David's body shook against his.

"We will," David told the woman, and he sounded as if he could barely keep from laughing. "Sorry for the inconvenience."

The door shut again and Zack stepped away slowly, but without breaking the contact completely. He kept one of his hands on the side of David's neck as he stared at him and took everything in — disheveled clothes, an obvious erection, red marks on his neck, puffed lips and half-opened eyes staring back at him.

He couldn't believe he had come so close to having sex in a freaking parking lot of a restaurant.

David tightened his grip on Zack's hips. "Your place then?"

"What?"

"I live with my brother. You live alone, right? I was hoping we'd finish what we started here."

Zack wanted to. He really, really wanted to, but his brain had started to come back on.

"I can't drive yet." He winced. His cock wasn't as hard as it had been a minute ago, but the ride would be far from comfortable.

And the heated look David sent his erection made his cock harden again.

"Stop that."

David bit down on his lower lip and Zack wanted his teeth there. *Damn it*. He looked away.

"Here's what I think," David said quietly, the rough edges of his lower voice smoothing out as he went. "We can load your bike in the back of my truck, and I can drive us both home. Then you get to decide if I'm going in with you or driving away. Or, we can split now and you can stay here and wait until you're fit to drive."

If the way his thumbs were rubbing circles onto Zack's skin was anything to go by, David was voting for the first option.

"Do you have things to secure my bike?"

David offered him a slow grin. "I'm a construction worker, Zack. I have almost everything in the back of my truck."

Zack nodded, making a decision. "Okay, then. Let's do this."

It took them just a few minutes to load and secure the bike, since David did indeed have everything they needed. They barely said anything, understanding each other easily, and soon they were sitting in the truck and David was backing out of the parking lot.

The desire had lost most of its urgency when they were interrupted then had to deal with the bike, but Zack could still feel the pull to kiss and bite every inch of David's body. He wanted to leave more marks on his neck, wanted to see him come.

"Not that I'm not enjoying this," David's voice was almost a growl as he pulled the window completely open, "but I do need to keep myself from crashing this truck, if only so it doesn't delay dragging you to bed."

It took a second for Zack to understand, then he took a deep breath and almost whined. Everything smelled like the two of them and sex, and neither of them had come even once yet. What were they going to smell like after that?

Cut it out, he told himself firmly, looking away. He needed to focus on something else for the rest of the trip, but it was hard when David was this close. Zack's wolf was restless now, seeking the satisfaction from earlier, and Zack's human side was in full agreement, if a little more patient — but only a little. He cursed his stupid idea to pick a place so far away from home.

Finally, they got there. Zack was out of the truck before David had even turned the engine off. They unloaded the bike quickly and Zack parked it in its usual place. When he turned back around, David was leaning against the side of his truck, looking at him with the same heat as before.

"So." David raised his eyebrows. "What is it going to be?"

There wasn't really a choice to be made.

"Follow me," Zack said and led him to his apartment building. If he touched David now, it could end in very public sex, and that was not what he wanted. Or rather, it wasn't what he wanted *right now*. The idea of one day claiming David in public... Zack closed his eyes for a second.

When they got to his apartment, they crashed into each other even before the door was fully closed. David ran his hands all over Zack's chest and shoulders, finally burying his fingers in his hair. He tugged at it hard and Zack's knees buckled as he swore into the skin of David's neck.

When they pulled back enough to be able to take their clothes off, they undressed quickly, leaving every piece where it fell. Zack caught David by his waist, spun him around then pushed him down onto the bed. He had a split second to commit the sight to memory — David spread on his bed, naked and hard — before following him and covering David's body with his own, moaning into his neck at the feel of naked skin against naked skin.

When they kissed, the same sizzling energy from the parking lot came back, the same need to get closer and closer. Now there was nothing separating them, nothing standing in their way.

David wrapped his arms around Zack, then moved his hands lower to grip his ass and pull Zack closer. That made their hard cocks slide against each other and Zack let out a half-moan, half-growl before getting up on his knees.

"Turn around," he said as he backed away so that David could roll onto his stomach. "I want your ass up, but your head low." He rubbed the back of David's thigh as he did what Zack told him to. "Perfect." He positioned himself right behind David and he had to bite down on his lip as his hard cock rubbed against David's ass. Zack leaned over him and licked a line up his spine before going back down, kissing and sucking until he reached his lower back. David was shuddering under him and Zack breathed in deeply. He could move farther, lick into him and spread him out around his tongue, make him ready before he fucked him hard. His mouth watered at the idea, but he shelved it for later. Now he just moved to one side and bit down on one of the ass cheeks, grinning when David swore into the pillow. He licked the reddened skin at the same time as he reached down between David's legs and gripped his balls.

"Fuck," the muffled curse came louder this time.

Zack trailed his hand up and down the side of David's leg. "What was that?"

David didn't answer him, so Zack tightened his grip on his balls.

"Fuck! I said 'fuck'."

"Ah." Zack grinned. "That's better. You should speak louder."

David pushed his ass back against Zack. "Will it make you fuck me sooner?"

"I don't know," he said, amused. He was loving the attitude. "It might."

"Come and fuck me then," David said loudly. Not screaming, but half-way there.

"Oh, I will." Zack dragged himself away from David to take out the lube. He paused. "No condom okay?"

"Ye-es."

Zack breathed out in relief. Most werewolves disliked condoms and since they couldn't catch any disease, they rarely needed to use them, but sometimes they were a personal preference anyway. He was glad David didn't ask for one, because Zack wanted his smell all over David. He wanted to mark him inside and out, without anything standing in his way.

He situated himself back behind David and again he took a second to commit this sight to the memory — David on his knees, with his ass up and face hidden in the pillow, the arch of his back tempting Zack to run his hands over it. And he was going to. Just not right now.

He opened the lube and poured it onto his palm, then tossed the container away. He lubed one finger of his other hand slowly, trying to catch his breath, but then David pushed back again and Zack couldn't wait anymore.

"Spread your legs."

David complied immediately. He also shifted his weight onto one arm and reached back with his other hand to spread his ass farther.

Zack couldn't hold back a moan. "Fuck, yes, just like that."

He reached out and circled the tip of his finger over David's hole, over and over, rubbing against the opening once in a while. Then he pushed the tip in, slowly at first, then faster when David's muscles relaxed and let him in, enveloping him in heat and pressure.

"Another," David breathed out.

"What? I didn't hear you."

"Give me another. I can take it."

Zack added lube onto his second and third finger before pushing them in—one, then soon after, the other. David was rocking back against him, pulling him deeper, and Zack had to close his other hand over the base of his cock to stop himself from coming.

"I'm ready. Come on."

Time for teasing was over. Zack pulled out his fingers, spread the lube over his cock, then moved to lean his body against David's. He thrust in, pushing inside until he bottomed out.

It was his turn to shudder—or maybe they both did. David's muscles hugged his cock perfectly, and the heat spread through Zack's entire body like a series of little electric shocks. He grasped David's hips for leverage, then started moving, pulling out a bit, only to slide back in, first slowly, then speeding up. The sounds of damp skin slapping against damp skin nearly drowned out Zack's harsh breathing and David's quiet, muffled moans. They fell into a rhythm almost from the start, then it was like they were racing to the finish line, pushing each other harder and harder. David countered Zack's every thrust with one of his own, and when David raised onto his elbows to gain more leverage, the angle change made Zack swear under his breath. Zack worked even harder, wanting to make him come, wanting to see if he could do that without touching his cock.

He did. After another sharp thrust, David moaned and dropped his head down, and the muscles closing around Zack's cock told him he'd gotten what he'd wanted. And that propelled him over the finish line as well, after a few more thrusts into David's tightened hole. When he came, he fell forward over David's back and he rested his forehead against it as he caught his breath. He licked David's dampened skin, seeking out even more of his taste. Zack took a deep breath and a pleased growl escaped from his throat at the scent of them, and sex, and sweat.

He was spent and sated, and his mind was quiet. He never wanted to move again.

Chapter Eight

David wasn't sure he could trust any of his muscles to hold him up right now. His body felt like jelly and he was just staring at the ceiling, waiting for the feeling to come back to his arms or legs so he could do anything other than rolling out from under Zack and turning onto his back.

Zack seemed to be in similar condition next to him, falling onto his back and sprawling over his side of the bed.

"That was…" David's own voice sounded weird to him, as if his vocal cords were half-ready to give up on him.

"Yeah."

Zack brushed the back of his hand against David's hip, so David gathered all his energy to turn his head and meet Zack's gaze.

"You wore me out," he said, laughter bubbling just beneath the surface.

One side of Zack's lips curled up. "I'm quite spent myself, if you haven't noticed."

David chuckled. "Let's call it even."

"Sure."

They fell into a comfortable silence, still looking at each other, but both floating in their own thoughts. David enjoyed a slight buzz of post-orgasmic crash, not really thinking of anything but how good he felt and how brown Zack's eyes were.

Sometime later, Zack rolled onto his side and propped himself on his elbow, looking down at David. He reached out and rubbed his thumb over David's lower lip.

"You make me wish I could go again right now."

David snorted. "Man, I'm not sure I will be able to go again tomorrow." He softened his smile. "But I know what you mean." He nipped at Zack's thumb to make his point.

Zack shook his head and pulled his hand back. "No teasing."

"Says the guy who was all, 'I can't hear you', twenty minutes ago?" David smirked. "Don't tell me about teasing."

Zack flashed his teeth in a predatory grin. "I'm not going to *tell* you…"

David bit his lower lip as a small shiver ran along his spine. "Okay, so maybe I won't need to wait until tomorrow."

The burst of laughter surprised David, but he stared, mesmerized, at the way Zack threw his head back and seemed to laugh with his whole body.

"Good to know," he finally said when he calmed down.

They stared at each other again and David really didn't want to move, but he was covered in quickly-drying bodily fluids, inside and out, and he needed a shower.

Zack rumbled in protest when he mentioned the bathroom, but David shook his head.

"Man, I have jizz dripping out of my body —"

For a guy who was completely spent just a moment ago, Zack could move incredibly fast. One second David was about to get up, and the next he was pinned down, with Zack lying half on top of him and pushing his thigh between his legs.

David blinked before smirking up at Zack. "You have some strong feelings against personal hygiene, don't you?"

Zack's gaze ran over his body and he opened his mouth to say something. Then he frowned and shut it, pulling back a little. David waited a few seconds, unsure what to do, but when nothing followed, he sat up.

"Be a good host and point me to the bathroom." When Zack indeed pointed to the door to the right, David leaned over and kissed him. "You can join me, if you want," he said, lips against lips.

Zack shook his head, but he ran a hand through David's hair and David tilted his head into the touch. "I would, but I'm pretty sure I'd fall and crack my skull open."

David scrunched his nose. "Lovely image."

"Not what you had in mind when you thought about me in the shower?"

He shook his head. He thought about Zack on his knees, swallowing him down — or vice-versa. David would love to suck Zack's cock at some point soon. "Maybe I'll tell you what I had in mind some other time." With that, he got up from the bed.

"Tease," he heard behind him and he sent a smirk over his shoulder, but closed the bathroom door quickly before the sight of Zack spread over the bed, with his hands behind his head, could make David run back to him.

"Shower," he whispered to himself. "Focus on the shower."

"What did you say?" Zack's amused voice came through the door. "I didn't hear you."

The flash of memory of the last time Zack used these words made David's dick twitch.

"Shut up, you tease," he shouted.

The laughter was his only answer and when he glanced into the mirror, David realized he was grinning.

* * * *

David hesitated before coming out of the bathroom, since there was a part of him that expected awkwardness. They had just had amazing sex, but what now? David knew he should be getting back to his apartment soon, but he wasn't in any hurry to leave Zack's place. He didn't want to break the bubble they were in, and he started to regret insisting on that shower. Dry semen was not too high a price for staying in bed with Zack.

Finally, he got out of the bathroom, and he came face to face with a fully-dressed Zack.

That went downhill pretty quickly, he thought, gripping the towel tighter around his waist.

"I got a call. I'm sorry," Zack said, catching his arm. When David glanced at him, he did look unhappy about it. Then the uniform registered.

"You're going to work?"

"Yeah, the wife of the guy on shift went to the hospital with appendicitis and she needs surgery."

"Ouch. Sorry." David got a move on. He grabbed his clothes and pulled them on quickly, not bothering to go back to the bathroom. It wasn't like Zack hadn't seen him naked. "Done," he said, turning back to Zack, who lifted his gaze from where he had most likely been staring at David's ass. "Really?" David asked, smiling and shaking his head at the same time. A wave of affection swept through him before he pushed it back.

"I'm taking every opportunity to appreciate the things I like." Zack smirked, but then he looked around and grabbed his keys. "You have everything?"

David checked his pockets one more time. "Yeah, we can go."

They were at the door when Zack turned and pulled him in, catching his lips in a bruising kiss. David found Zack's hips, but before he could bring them closer, Zack took a step back.

"I really have to go."

Outside, Zack didn't touch him at all, just told him he would call, then he was off, backing his bike out onto the street. David watched him go and when Zack disappeared behind the corner, he got into his truck and drove home.

When he paused at the red light, he glanced in the rear-view mirror. Anybody who looked at him would have no problem guessing how he'd spent his evening. He was pretty sure some of those marks on his neck would still be there tomorrow.

"Masters of subtlety, we are not," David muttered to himself. But did they have to be? He didn't mind other people knowing, especially since he was hoping for a repeat performance — more than one, actually. He was hoping he would get to keep seeing Zack, because now that he'd had him once, he wouldn't be satisfied with a one-night stand.

But regardless of what he wanted, he hadn't discussed it with Zack yet, so David decided to keep it quiet until they talked about it. Hopefully soon.

He knew Charlie was definitely going to comment on the marks when he saw them. David would have to tell him something, but when he walked into their apartment, he still didn't know what that 'something' would be.

"Hey." He put the keys on the shelf next to the door.

Charlie was watching TV and he didn't turn as he answered in kind. David might have a shot at slipping past him unnoticed tonight.

That shot was lost when the commercial started playing on the screen a moment later and Charlie stood up and gathered his plate and glass. The kitchenette was right next to the front door and there was no way he wouldn't so much as glance at David in passing.

"Did you eat?" Charlie started, but then he looked at David and stopped. Full-body stopped, right there between the living room, the kitchenette and the entrance, staring at David as if he'd gotten a tattoo on his forehead.

David looked down and pulled off his shoes. "I ate, thanks."

"You look like someone ate *you*," Charlie told him, and David rolled his eyes.

"Seriously?"

"Have you seen you?"

"Have I... Yes, I've seen me. I look like a guy who enjoyed himself tonight."

Charlie made a face. "Spare me."

"Do we have to go over that 'yes, big brother, I have sex on occasion' conversation again?" David crossed his arms against his chest. "Because it wasn't fun the first time."

"No, we don't." Charlie put down the dishes in the sink and crossed his arms, mirroring David. "I just don't want to hear the details. You wouldn't want to hear about my sex life, would you?"

"Do you even have one?"

As soon as the words were out of his mouth, David regretted them, but it was too late. Charlie narrowed his eyes for a moment, then he shook his head. "Whether I do or not, I wouldn't talk to you about it, just like you don't really want to talk to me about this." He made a circling gesture in David's direction. "So how about I go back to my movie, and we'll see each other tomorrow."

Charlie turned around before he headed back to the couch, and David was left feeling like an asshole. He ran a hand through his hair and went to his room, replaying their fight over and over in his head. He'd gotten what he wanted when Charlie hadn't pushed him for anything and, instead of being happy, David had turned the tables and gotten in his face about it. Then he'd made that below-the-belt comment about Charlie's sex life. What the hell was wrong with him?

He undressed, brushed his teeth, then got into bed. Staring up at his ceiling, he tried to forget about the fight. They did that from time to time—blew up over something stupid then let it go, pretended it hadn't happened. But this one felt particularly shitty, because David had crossed a line and he knew it. He had no idea when the topic of the lack of sex in Charlie's life had become a subject they both actively avoided, but it had happened nevertheless. Throwing it in Charlie's face like that was not something David was proud of.

He rubbed his eyes and tried to think of something else. His mind, predictably, turned to Zack. David recalled lying in bed next to him after sex, spent and loose—and happy. He touched the side of his neck where most of his marks were, and, as he rubbed the sensitive skin, the heat radiating from it sent a wave of warm comfort through David's body. He closed his eyes. He might not know what he was doing with Zack and where it was going, but he would enjoy it while it lasted.

He would enjoy it for however long Zack would let him.

Chapter Nine

Zack had a long, quiet night at the station to think about him and David, but as the first rays of sunshine came through the windows, he was just as clueless as he'd been when he'd gotten there.

He stared at his reflection in the bathroom mirror, unsettled by the fact that he had no visible marks after his time with David. Zack had left his—damn, he'd basically mauled David's neck—but he had barely a few scratches over his hip. That was it.

You wouldn't want one, he told himself, *not where others could see*. And it was true. He would freak out over even one hickey, because people would notice and that was the last thing he wanted. And yet...

He shook his head. Last night hadn't been like anything he'd expected. From the fact that they'd almost had sex in the restaurant's parking lot, to the way David had felt right in his bed, even after sex... All of that was something new, and Zack had no idea what to do.

After he left the station, he stopped at the diner for a quick breakfast. There weren't a lot of people there since it was still early in the morning, but a few heads turned and he received a few nods. No one did a double-take. No one made a joke about long, hard nights. *Which was good*, Zack reminded himself.

"What it's gonna be, sweetie?" Chloe asked from behind the counter. "Scrambled eggs with bacon?"

"You know it." He sat down at the stool and nodded his thanks as she poured him coffee. "Thank you."

"Anything for a handsome man in uniform." She winked at him and he couldn't help but smile. She was old enough to be his mother, and she'd busted him more than once when he'd skipped classes back in high school and had wanted to hang out there.

Then the diner's doors opened and Zack didn't have to turn around to sense Taylor behind him.

"Another night shift?" Taylor put a hand on his shoulder and, damn, the touch made Zack lose half the tension he'd been gathering in the last few hours. Taylor had been settling into the role of the Alpha's Son since he'd been back in Harrington Hills for good, and it seemed to strengthen his powers. Or maybe it was the effect of mating. Who knew?

"Yeah, last minute thing." Zack tilted his chin at the stool next to him. "You want to join me?"

"Sure."

Chloe poured Taylor coffee as well, then got his order before moving to the other end of the counter.

"What are you doing here so early?" Zack asked, glancing at the clock on the wall. It was only quarter past eight.

"I dropped Kevin off at Kath and Chin's place. They wanted a pre-baby photo session." Taylor took a sip of coffee. "And I have a meeting with the zoning committee in less than an hour. I need carbs."

"Ah." Half of the zoning committee were human, and since they didn't have to adhere to the pack's hierarchy, they liked to show off their independence from time to time, making trouble for all the locals with bullshit restrictions that didn't really lead anywhere. Zack didn't envy his cousin having to deal with those people at all.

"And what's up with you? How are things?" Taylor asked.

How are they indeed. Zack didn't really know. "Things are fine," he finally said, because 'I'm wondering if I should text the guy I slept with last night' sounded lame, even to him.

"Good. You look better than at the party."

Zack just nodded. He *felt* better than at the party, but he was still confused.

"Should I just stop talking?" Taylor didn't sound irritated, more like someone who didn't care either way.

"Yeah," came Zack's quiet reply and that was it, the conversation was over.

They ate in silence for a few minutes and he found himself gradually relaxing again. It could be from Taylor backing off or from his power to influence pack members, but whatever it was, it worked, and Zack sighed in relief.

The words tumbled out of him when he was finished with his food and Taylor was down to the last pancake. "I gave it a try."

Thankfully Taylor seemed to catch on immediately. "And?"

"And I don't know what's next." Zack shrugged, pushing his plate away and leaning his elbows on the counter.

"Do what feels right and don't overthink it. If you spend all your time going over every possible scenario, you'll never do anything." Taylor licked the syrup off his thumb. "You don't have to know what's going to happen a month from now. Go at it one day at the time."

"Easier said than done." One day of being seen with each other in public meant at least a month of gossip — of hearing everyone's opinion about him and David.

"In the infinite wisdom of your pack's Alpha, 'tough shit'." Taylor smirked. "This is what I got when I went to her for advice on Kevin." Then he grew serious again. "But whatever you do, don't leave him hanging. Text him or call him. Sometimes people are insecure in ways you don't think about, and a little reassurance is good."

Zack nodded. David didn't seem like an insecure guy at all, but Taylor was right. It wasn't always obvious. Zack would bet most people probably wouldn't believe half the shit going through his own mind.

Taylor finished his coffee and left the money under the cup. He was about the get up when he paused and leaned closer to Zack. "One more thing. Don't run away because you're scared," he said quietly. "If you don't want him, that's a different story, but if you think of running because you do want him, but you came up with some bullshit reasons not to take the chance? Just don't." Then he got up and clasped his hand on Zack's shoulder again, this time lingering a little longer. "Don't let him walk away because you think you can't have him," he whispered, barely audible, and stepped back. "I have to go," he added in a normal voice, before nodding at someone behind Zack's back. Then he left.

Zack stared at the door for a minute before going back to the rest of his coffee. He pulled out his phone and, before he could talk himself out of it, he typed in a quick text to David.

Hi, how are you? I'm sorry for cutting the evening short last night. I'd love to make it up to you.

He clicked Send before he could overthink it and winced as he reread it right after. 'How are you?' Really? He put his phone back into his pocket and got up from the stool. It was time to go home to get some sleep.

* * * *

He woke up after one p.m. and rubbed his hands over his eyes. He'd only caught a few hours, but he felt more rested than usual. His sleep cycle had to be whacked again, but he had no night shifts for the next week and a half, so he would get it back to normal.

He reached for his phone without looking, and there was a text from David, sent three hours earlier.

Hi. :) Last night was great before you had to go, so you're forgiven. But you can make it up to me anyway. ;) I'm free every day after 6:30.

Zack hit Reply.

Tonight, then? Seven at my place? I make great burgers.

Great! I realized today I can walk from the house to your place. If you don't mind lending me your shower again, I could come straight to yours after I'm done here.

Zack pictured David coming out from his bathroom in nothing but a towel the previous night.

I'll gladly let you use my shower any time.

Good to know. ;) See you tonight!

Zack reread the last few texts and smiled. Taking things one day at a time might work.

He rolled out of bed then stretched, looking around. He lived in a studio apartment, so there wasn't a lot of space, but he thought it suited him perfectly. He needed to clean it up today, though, because even if David had seen the mess last night and didn't care, tonight it would be different. Tonight was planned, so Zack had to make some effort.

After a quick lunch, he started cleaning and, as he was sorting clothes and gathering up the dishes, he couldn't help thinking about him and David. But instead of worrying about what might be, he tried to focus on the good stuff—on how great last night had been, even before the sex—on how David fit right against him, how responsive he was, how he gave as much as he got, how Zack seemed to get high on his scent, seemed to crave it more and more.

His sheets smelled of both of them and he hesitated before pulling them off. Then he realized how ridiculous he was and stripped the bed quickly. If the evening went as he hoped it would, the new sheets were going to smell like them anyway. Zack grinned at the thought as he took his laundry bag and smiled all the way to the laundry room.

* * * *

By the time David sent him a text that he was on his way, the apartment was cleaner than it had been in months. Zack wouldn't call himself a slob, but clothes thrown all over the place didn't usually bother him unless there was someone coming over, and he hadn't had guests in... He couldn't even remember. Taylor and Kevin had come over soon after they'd moved out here to stay, so about two months ago. There had been no one since then.

With the pack meeting at various events every weekend or so, Zack didn't really socialize much outside of that. And before last night, he hadn't had sex in far too long to even think about.

The intercom rang right as he was taking the meat out of the fridge. He let David in and dried his hands on the kitchen towel. When he heard footsteps right outside his door, he opened it without waiting for a knock.

David's clothes were speckled with paint and probably plaster, and he had a gym bag slung over his shoulder. He grinned as Zack waved him inside. "Hi."

"Hi." Zack closed the door before grabbing him and turning them both around so he could back David up against the wall.

They were both grinning when they kissed, so it was chaste at first, but then David licked the corner of Zack's mouth and a moment later they were grasping at each other and deepening the kiss. When Zack pushed one of his hands under the back of David's T-shirt and ran it over the slightly damp skin, he moaned and rolled his hips forward.

David pulled his head back. "I told you I need a shower," he said, sounding like he wanted to laugh but was too out of breath to do so. "I'm making you filthy." He didn't take his hands off Zack's hips though.

"I think we can get filthier before you get into the shower." Zack lowered his head and licked a long line from David's collarbone to his jaw. The scent and taste, stronger after the day of hard work, made Zack crazy with want.

Then suddenly they were spinning around and before he knew what happened, David had pinned him against the wall with a wicked grin. He had one hand splayed over Zack's chest, keeping him in place. "Fine by me," he whispered, before falling down onto his knees.

Damn. Zack had to close his eyes for a moment, because the sight of David kneeling in front of him, with his head so close to Zack's cock straining against the zipper and with his teasing smile as he looked up at him...

"You'd better open up those beautiful eyes or you're going to miss quite a show," David said, and Zack did as he was told. He watched David opening his jeans and almost choked on air as David leaned closer to inhale deeply, right next to Zack's erection. "You smell so good." The muffled voice was barely audible, but Zack still heard him.

You too, he wanted to say. *You smell amazing, and I didn't get enough.* Then David shoved Zack's jeans and underwear down to his knees, and his every thought disappeared. There was only David's grip on his hips, David's tongue on his cock, the sounds he was making as he sucked Zack almost all the way down.

Zack's hand landed on the back of David's head and he pushed it closer. It was light and David could've easily resisted, but he didn't. He moaned around Zack's cock and managed to lean against his hand, his touch, without taking his mouth off Zack.

Taking it as a permission, Zack did it again, a little harder, and David relaxed against it, lifting his gaze back up to meet Zack's. His orgasm started to build and he shoved his cock deep into David's mouth, hitting the back of his throat, then pulled back only to do it again. They didn't look away from each other and Zack was biting his lip hard enough to taste blood. Then David gave him an almost invisible nod, and that was it. Zack came with a shuddering breath and it seemed to last forever as he slumped against the wall and David kept licking him and sucking, swallowing every last drop.

"Up," Zack breathed out finally. "Come up."

As soon as David was standing, Zack pulled him into a kiss, licking into his swollen lips and seeking out his own taste on David's tongue, the mix he became immediately addicted to. He reached for David's cock, cupping it through the material of his jeans and gripping tightly.

"Oh," David choked and leaned forward, hands braced against the wall on both sides of Zack's head.

"That's it," Zack whispered, cheek smashed against David's as he whispered, rubbing his hand back and forth. "You're so close. Just come like this."

And David did. He shuddered before falling forward and trapping Zack's hand between them.

Neither of them said anything for a long moment, and Zack brushed his nose against David's shoulder as David caught his breath. Their mixed scent made Zack inhale deeply. His mind was blissfully empty.

Chapter Ten

David ended up showering alone, after all.

"I'm sure you can get me back for that later," Zack told him with a smirk. "Meanwhile, I'm going to take care of the burgers, and you'd better go clean up."

So he did. He shouldered the gym bag he'd dropped earlier then headed for the bathroom. He'd grabbed what he needed from his car before he'd left it at the house. It didn't make sense to drive two blocks and risk catching unwanted attention.

He sighed in relief as he pulled his dirty clothes off. After a whole day of patching up holes in the walls and painting the kitchen, his muscles were sore, and the blow job he'd given Zack hadn't helped. *It was worth it, though*, he thought with a smirk.

He ran the water as hot as he could stand it and let out a moan as the spray hit his shoulders and back. For a minute he just stood there, enjoying the water massage, then he thought of the guy outside the bathroom door and reached for a shower gel. The quicker he was done here, the faster he could get back to Zack.

* * * *

The burgers were amazing.

David swallowed the last bite as he reached out for his beer. "They're really good."

"I know," Zack said with a chuckle. "You've told me that three times already."

"Well, they are that good."

"Noted."

They grinned at each other across the table-slash-kitchen island and David wanted to reach out and grab Zack's hand in his. He didn't. Instead he straightened his left leg and nudged Zack's foot as he sat back in his chair.

"Are you playing footsie with me?" Zack asked, but he dropped his legs to the sides, brushing his calf over the top of David's foot.

"I don't know. Is it working?"

Zack snorted. "I feel like I'm back in high school."

"I didn't do that in high school." David wiggled his eyebrows. "But I did other things we could do."

Something crossed Zack's face like a shadow, here in one second and gone the next, but before David could ask, Zack shook his head and stood up.

"Leave your glory days in the past and let's move to the couch. How about that?"

David had a retort ready about necking on the couch being most definitely a part of his high school history, but he let it go. Maybe Zack, being older and all, didn't want to think about David being even younger than he was now, which was more than fine with him.

When they'd settled on the couch, close, but barely touching, Zack suggested a crime show David was vaguely familiar with. He agreed as he burrowed back into the couch cushions with a contented sigh. He was comfortable, full of good food, and he had a guy next to him whom he—

Uh-oh. He froze with his beer bottle half-way to his mouth. He lowered his hand and stared at the screen without really seeing anything.

A guy *whom he was falling for.* That was where his inner monologue was going. He didn't really know what to do with that thought. The rational part of his mind—the one that sounded as if Charlie wrote its script—protested that it was too early to tell, that no one really fell that quickly. Like? Yes. Want? Yes. Hell, lust over? Sure. But fall in love?

How much time do you really need, though? the less-rational part jumped in. *A week? Two? A month? Six months?*

David glanced at Zack, who was focused on the screen. Whatever it was and however it felt, he shouldn't get his hopes up too high—at least for now.

He made himself look at the TV. He was comfortable, well-fed, in good company, and there was a pretty big chance he'd be having sex later on. That was more than enough.

* * * *

"We'll miss the part where they reveal the killer," he told Zack, who was mouthing at his neck and pushing him onto his back, but David's protest probably didn't appear very convincing since his hands were under Zack's T-shirt, roaming up and down his spine.

"The flight attendant did it," Zack murmured against his ear, right as he ran his hand down David's chest and stomach.

"What? Why?" David asked, suddenly distracted, but when Zack looked at him with a frown, he burst out laughing. "Sorry." He pulled him against his body. "You'll tell me later."

Zack made a point of reaching for a remote and turning the TV off with a huff, and David had to bite his lip not to laugh at him again. The laughter turned into a sigh as Zack lifted David's T-shirt up to his armpits and started to kiss and lick the exposed skin. When he flicked his tongue over David's left nipple, David bucked his hips, but Zack's body kept him down. He couldn't do much more than run his hands over Zack's shoulders and the back of his neck, occasionally slipping them into his hair. He tugged at the loose strands when Zack sucked his nipple into his mouth, but Zack's only response was to latch on with his teeth, and that sent a full-body shudder through David.

He dropped his legs open even more and rested one foot on the floor. Suddenly Zack was covering most of his body, and David's wolf preened.

"Let's move this to the bed." Zack pulled back and scrambled to his feet, and David had two seconds to feel the loss of warmth over his body before there was a hand right in front of his face. He clasped it and let himself be pulled up, but before he let Zack's hand go, he brought it to his lips and brushed a kiss over his knuckles.

He took a step back then grabbed the hem of his shirt. He yanked it off quickly, then tossed it onto the couch. Looking straight at Zack, who didn't take his gaze away from him, David shoved his jeans and boxers down until they were off, along with his socks. Still maintaining eye contact with Zack, he lobbed the pile of discarded clothing, and it landed on the couch as well. Then David stood completely naked right in front of Zack, who was still fully clothed. It made David's cock harden even more, and Zack licked his lips as he glanced down.

David reached out to grasp Zack's T-shirt, but Zack shook his head.

"Go lie down in the middle of the mattress, hands under your head. On your back," he added and David smiled, pleased. He wanted to see Zack.

He crossed the room, trembling minutely, hyper-aware of being watched. Then he turned and lay down on his back, pushed the pillow under his head and shoved his hands between the pillow and the mattress, all without taking his gaze off Zack, who seemed content to stand there and watch him.

But watching wasn't enough for David. He pushed one of his legs up and to the side, exposing himself more, and he would have been nervous about it if he weren't so turned on, looking at Zack right now. Zack's eyes flashed to his wolf eyes for a split second and the hands on his belt had claws. When David's gaze met Zack's again, he felt his own eyes flash too, and he tilted his head back, arching from the bed for more — more touch, more Zack, more everything.

He heard the sounds of clothes being pulled off, but he didn't look, staring at the wall above the bed, feeling his body aching and tingling. Then the bed dipped, and a moment later Zack's body was covering his and he let out a shaky exhale, pushing up and shamelessly rubbing himself against Zack. He forgot he was supposed to keep his hands under the pillow. He threw them around Zack's shoulders to pull him closer and closer. He strained his head up and licked and nipped low on Zack's neck, sucking a mark there, just like Zack was doing, right under David's ear.

Everything seemed too hot, and their skin was slick with sweat, making it hard to grasp and hold on to anything. David might have let out a quiet whine, but then Zack's mouth was there, swallowing every sound David made, and they kissed for so long that David's lips felt numb when they finally parted.

"How soon can you get in me?" David asked, dragging fingers up Zack's neck and into the hair at the back of his head.

"Not soon enough." Zack slid down David's body again, kissing and licking, and David tightened his grip on the sheets as he tried to catch his breath. Zack moved away for a moment to get the lube, then he was back, mouthing at David's hip before moving down along his groin, licking and grazing with his teeth from time to time. He didn't touch David's cock at all. Instead he moved to suck another mark on the inside of his thigh while he used lubed fingers to find David's hole.

There was no teasing like last night. Zack went right in and kept a fast pace, adding more fingers as soon as David breathed out, "More." When Zack finally slid inside him, David let out a long moan as the hot sparks went off over his whole body.

Zack leaned over him, supporting himself on his elbows on both sides of David's head. They locked eyes and everything outside of this, *them*, dropped out of focus. It seemed as if neither of them even blinked. They kept staring at each other the entire time, even as Zack started to push into him harder, even as David remembered how to move and pushed back against Zack's thrusts. The air was so heavy with their scent that David could almost taste it.

His orgasm seemed to be building in waves, but he finally came right after Zack, spurting into almost non-existent space between their bodies. It took a while for him to dial down his senses from the high, and the contentment spread through him as he became aware Zack was nuzzling his neck.

After a couple of minutes, Zack slipped out of him before moving to the side. He stayed close, leaning over David, and ran his hand up and down David's chest and stomach.

"Are you spreading my own jizz all over me?" David asked after a minute. He felt one corner of his mouth quirking up.

Zack shrugged. "I like your scent. I like how you wear both yours and mine."

David nodded. He liked it, too. And they could both enjoy it for now.

Chapter Eleven

Zack didn't want to wake up. He was floating in the perfect state of light sleep, where he was warm, comfortable and aware he was curled up around another body—a body that smelled like him and his. He didn't want to move at all.

The choice was taken out of his hands when an unfamiliar melody started playing somewhere by the couch and suddenly Zack was pushed back and the body—David—stumbled out of bed.

"Hello," David's low, raspy voice made Zack smile, but then he frowned when he realized David wasn't talking to him. He lifted his head to see him standing naked by the couch and rubbing his eyes with his free hand. "Oh, hey, Jack."

That Zack liked even less.

"No, no, I remember, I just— Yeah, I overslept. It's totally fine. Of course you can come. I told you. Sure, okay. See you at noon."

David smiled when he finished the call, but Zack's consolation was the way his smile grew tenfold when David's gaze landed on him.

"Sorry for the wake-up call. Well, sorry for waking *you* up. I've overslept, so Jack actually did me a favor."

In his still half-asleep brain, Zack couldn't see how dragging David away from him was a good thing — a favor, even.

He was awake enough to know he was going to be embarrassed by his thoughts later on, but he couldn't help it. At least he managed to keep his mouth shut.

"You awake?" David said, quieter this time, gentler, as he walked back to the bed's edge.

"Some," Zack mumbled and David chuckled.

"I wish I could stay for longer, but I'm already late. I need to finish the hall today and now Jack's coming over to check out the place, so I have even less time."

"Could I get a tour, too?" Zack asked before he could stop himself, but David seemed pleased — surprised, but pleased.

"Sure. Do you want to come by with Jack?"

Zack shook his head. There was a part of him that would love to be there when Jack came over, but he realized how stupid that was.

"Some other time, maybe?" He leaned up on his elbows. "I'd love a private showing."

David chuckled. "Then maybe we should wait until the furniture arrives. My back may hate me otherwise."

"I'm sure we could make it work."

"I'm sure we could." David leaned over and kissed him, even if the kiss wasn't nearly long enough. "I need to get dressed and go. You get some more sleep, if you want, then text me. We'll figure out our plans."

Zack blinked. He realized David framed it in a way that both extended the invitation for contact and left Zack enough room to back out if he wanted to.

But he didn't want that. He didn't want that at all.

"Okay. I'll text you. You sure you don't need anything? Breakfast? Coffee?" Zack needed to be a good host.

"No, thanks. No time for that."

David pulled on his clothes quickly, grabbed his bag and was out of the door before Zack managed to get out of bed. With his apartment now empty and no plans for the immediate future, Zack fell back against the pillows. *Just a half an hour more.*

* * * *

Three messages were waiting for him when he woke up — one from his mother, asking him if he would come over tonight and two from David.

Jack invited me for a beer with his friends tonight and said you could come too, if you want, so I'm extending the invitation.

Yeah, he guessed, but he's not going to tell anyone, if you're worried about it.

Zack sighed. He'd intended to say no to his mother, hoping for more time with David, but he had no desire to go out with Jack and his friends. It would be too weird, and this was not how he wanted the town to find out about him and David.

Not that he had any idea of how he wanted to do it, but still…not like this.

Thanks, but I'll pass. Mom reminded me I should show up at her place tonight.

He got a reply right away.

Sure. Something wrong?

No, it's my stepfather's birthday today, and I forgot.

Got it. Well, I'm free any other evening, so just let me know when you want to meet. :)

Zack was both excited and nervous about David's easy acceptance and open invitation. The guy kept surprising him daily, and he didn't know how to deal with that, how to make sense of it. Zack was happy when they were together, but whenever he was left alone to think, he started having doubts. And whenever he was unsure about something, his instincts made him back off.

He wrote his mother that he would make an appearance, and he tried to cheer himself up with the thought that there was a guarantee of great food and getting his share of leftovers. He would survive one evening. He wasn't a whiny teenager with a big chip on his shoulder anymore. He even liked his stepfather now, after he'd left all his resentment behind when he'd decided to finally grow up. He could make an effort.

* * * *

The evening had been fine, in the end. Far from the worst it had ever been, but Zack could admit that he'd used to cause most of the drama himself. He'd been a clichéd kid who acted out because his younger siblings had a father who cared, while his had bailed before Zack was even born. He'd acted out because Tia and Ted didn't, and because his mother kept trying with him, and because his stepfather did, too, against all odds.

And sure, Zack had grown out of that, but he still couldn't truly relax at this table. This was why he rarely visited, content to meet at various pack gatherings instead — less trouble for everyone involved and less irritation on his part.

Zack and Tia had been mostly fine in recent years, but they would both agree they had little in common. Ted, on the other hand, grated on Zack's nerves more and more. Tonight, for example, Ted had shared with them that he was thinking of taking a year off from college and going on an adventure, which would be fine, if he hadn't still been expecting his parents to keep paying for everything. When his father told him no, Ted turned to Mom for help. Then everyone started fighting.

By the time they'd all calmed down again and Mom had asked what was going on in Zack's life, the last thing he wanted was to share any of his problems. *I'm sleeping with a guy almost a decade younger, and I don't know what to do with it,* he imagined telling them then snorted at the mere idea.

"What's so funny?" his mom asked.

He shook his head. "Nothing. I'm good. Everything is good. I've just had two night shifts in a row, so I'm a little tired, but that's all."

"Double night shift?" His mom frowned.

"It was an emergency. One of the guys couldn't show up, so I was called in. Usually we have a night shift two or three times a month," he added to remind her. She'd been very proud when he'd joined the sheriff's department, but she also worried about his job, and while he could understand some of that worry, most of it was completely unnecessary.

"Harrington Hills isn't exactly a high-level crime area, Mom," Ted said. "And Zack has pulled all-nighters before." He smirked at Zack. "Many of them, I'm sure."

Zack grimaced. "Yeah, because that's exactly the same thing."

"I'm sure they're more boring now, but since you're getting old—"

"If he's getting old, what does that make me?" Zack's stepfather raised his eyebrows at his son.

Ted grinned. "I'm not sure you really want me to answer that, Dad."

"You're right. I don't."

They spent the rest of the dinner bickering, but it wasn't malicious and the tension from earlier was gone. Zack managed to actually enjoy himself a bit.

It wasn't until later, when he was loading the plates into the dishwasher and his mom was packing the leftovers for him, that she cleared her throat before asking, "Zack, are you seeing someone?"

He shoved the door of the dishwasher shut, probably a little too forcefully.

"What? Why?" There were a thousand possible answers running through his head, and he couldn't decide what to do. He'd let his guard down, and she'd surprised him. He wasn't ready.

"I'm curious," she said.

"I think the pack would know if I was dating someone, Mom," Zack told her, somehow managing to hide the truth in a different truth. Whatever he and David were doing, he wouldn't call that dating. They had gone on one date. The rest was... The rest was complicated.

"Kalinda told me yesterday that she thought she saw you at that restaurant near the northern city limits, but she wasn't sure it was you." She shook her head. "I told her it's not your usual place, since it's so far away, but I thought I would ask."

Zack raised his eyebrows. "Pretty roundabout way of asking me if I was in a restaurant." He worked really hard not to show his reaction, but he wasn't sure how much his mom was seeing.

"Why would you be there, if not for a date?"

"Well, I was there once, as we were coming back from Linwood with Portia. But it was months ago." Another truth.

"Can't you find yourself a boyfriend, though?" His mom put another jar into the bag for him.

"And here I was hoping for one night without that question," Zack said, dropping his shoulders. "Let it be, Mom."

"I want what's good for you."

What's good for him. Zack tried to imagine David here, at her table, tried to imagine her face when he told her whom he was sleeping with. He would bet money and all his leftovers that she would not be happy. David might be the newest darling of the town, but Zack's mother would focus on how young he was — how much younger than Zack.

And Zack wouldn't even blame her, since he kept coming back to the same issue himself, whenever he was alone. He kept picturing himself at David's age, only just leaving his rebellion behind and trying to make something of himself. What his younger self definitely hadn't done was look for a serious boyfriend, someone to settle down with. It had been a plan for the future, for a time when his life would be where he'd wanted it to be.

For a time like now, Zack thought. He just found it hard to believe that a guy eight years younger than him would be ready to settle down as well.

He was getting in the car twenty minutes later when he got a text from David.

If I drunk dial you later on, don't answer. I'm not planning to, but just in case.

Zack sighed.

And how do I know you're drunk dialing me and not calling for help or something?

You're right. So answer, but if I'm just drunk, don't listen to anything I say.

I didn't know you were planning to get smashed.

I wasn't, but Jack is very convincing.

Stupid jealousy roared inside of him, making his irritation even worse.

Okay.

When nothing came after that, he shoved his phone back in his pocket then drove off.

Chapter Twelve

David woke up at eight-thirty and rubbed his eyes, trying to will himself to get up and start the day. He had no plans before ten, when he was picking Jack up, but he could hear Charlie moving in the kitchen, so he decided to drag himself out of bed. They saw each other mostly in passing lately, and even though they'd put their last fight behind them, it would still be a good opportunity to spend some time together.

After a quick shower, he went to the kitchen and saw Charlie sitting at the table with his tablet and coffee.

"Hey," David said, going straight to the coffee maker. "Did you eat already?"

"Hey. Yeah, I did, I need to leave in half an hour or so."

David nodded. He pulled out eggs and milk from the fridge. "So no omelet for you, then?"

"No, thanks."

He asked Charlie about his work while he was preparing his breakfast. It suddenly reminded David of the old days of late dinners when his brother would tell him crazy stories from his different jobs. His current position at the library wasn't all that exciting, but it suited Charlie pretty well.

"What are you smiling about?" the man in question asked, after David sat down with his food.

"Nothing, just remembered something," he said, but when Charlie kept staring at him, David frowned. "What?"

"How was your evening last night?"

David smiled again. "Good, good. Jack introduced me to some of his friends, which was cool. Too many people in the pack are just faces to me, you know? I want to get to know more of them." He shrugged. "And it was nice to kick back and let loose."

One corner of Charlie's mouth tilted up. "Should I be glad you made it home in one piece?"

"I wasn't that drunk. But Jack's older brother dropped me off when he came to pick Jack up."

Charlie was about to take a sip of his coffee, but he paused at that. "The pack's future Alpha got you a ride home from a drunken night out?"

"Yes." David rolled his eyes. "He's not the Alpha yet. He's just a guy."

"And Jack?"

"What about him?"

"Is Jack 'just a guy'?"

David frowned. "He's my friend."

"A friend you sleep with?" Charlie asked, and David choked on his omelet.

"No," he told his brother firmly after clearing his throat. "I'm not sleeping with Jack."

"Because if you're hiding it because he's a Harrington—"

"I don't care what his last name is. I'm *not* sleeping with Jack." He shook his head. *Unbelievable.* "And it's the twenty-first century. There are no royals and commoners or whatever."

"The pack's hierarchy isn't—"

"It's Zack, okay?" David spat out, and he felt his shoulders drop. He hadn't planned on telling Charlie today, especially not like this, but now that it was out there, it was a relief. He didn't like keeping things from his brother.

Of course, one of the reasons he hadn't told him earlier was Charlie's inevitable reaction.

"Zack?" Charlie paused, probably going over every pack member he knew, searching for more than one Zack. Then he narrowed his eyes. "Harrington?"

"Yes. And don't worry. He's not an heir to the Alpha throne," David tried to lighten the mood, but his brother had nothing of it.

"Zack's ten years older than you!"

"He's eight years older, actually." David rubbed his hand over his temple. "And we're both adults."

Charlie crossed his arms against his chest. "Being an adult doesn't mean the same thing when you are years apart, especially at that age."

"Whose age?"

"Yours. It's—"

"How many times have you told me that I'm not a typical person for my age? I've been hearing that for years, but only when it suits you." David sat back in his chair and crossed his arms against his chest as well.

"Damn it. Don't tell me you don't see the big gap here." Charlie leaned on his forearms on the table. "You can see it—or maybe he can—because there's a reason no one knows about it."

"Or maybe *you* don't know, because I knew you'd act like this."

David almost wished he could take it back as soon as he'd said it, but he was still angry, so it was only 'almost'.

Charlie inhaled sharply, but he didn't back down. "Fine. Maybe someone more worthy of your honesty knows, but most of the pack doesn't. And you can tell me it's all on me — on how I would react — but it's not. If you don't think the gap is too big, then at least Zack does. And if he still sleeps with you in spite of it —"

"Stop it, Charlie," David cut in, suddenly out of patience. "How many times do I have to remind you that you don't make decisions for me anymore?"

"I'm not making any decision for you. But as your older brother —"

"Exactly. You're my older brother. You have to stop treating me like a child, at some point." David sighed. "Listen. You've done more for me than any average brother has to do. You took on a job of a guardian and you made it work, even if it was way too much to put on a twenty-one-year-old. I wish you could've gotten the life you should've had. I wish you could've gone on that tour you were supposed to go —"

"I wouldn't change a thing about that time." Charlie shook his head. "I wish our lives had been easier, but I have no regrets about being your guardian, and you know it."

David bit his lower lip. "I know. I know. And I'm thankful. But I'm not a kid anymore. I've been an adult a few years now, and I might not be enough of an adult to you — which is hypocritical, by the way, since you were younger than I am now when you became my guardian — but that's your opinion. I get to make my own decisions."

"You act like I gave you a hard time about every decision you've ever made, and that's not fair."

"Every decision you didn't agree with," David corrected. "Not going to college, having two jobs, starting the company—"

Charlie frowned. "I wasn't against you starting your company. What are you talking about?"

"You've had a list of things that could go wrong."

"Of course I did and so should you. You needed to be prepared, but that wasn't me being against it."

David sighed. "Fine. You weren't against it. But you were against other things, and now you're against Zack."

"I have nothing against Zack personally, but he's way, way older than you. It rarely works, especially at such a young age. And the way you're hiding it from everyone shows that you know it's an issue, too."

"Or maybe we're hiding it because it's still new, we don't know what it is yet, and we don't want the whole town to gossip."

Charlie looked at him for a long moment. "Is that your reason?"

It had been, at the start. Now, David knew that he wanted this thing between him and Zack to become more, and that meant he didn't care about hiding it any longer. But they hadn't had that talk yet, and David wasn't going to have it with his brother first. "Yes."

Charlie nodded. "Just make sure his reasons are the same." He looked at his mug before glancing up at David again. "You may think I baby you, and maybe I still do it from time to time, but it's not about that. Not just about that," he corrected when David shook his head. "Talk to him and make sure, so you'll know as well."

"I intend to," David told his brother before getting up. "I have to go. I'm meeting with Jack soon."

"Okay," Charlie said quietly to his back. David wished he could say something more, but lately both of them seemed to keep getting it wrong, so he wasn't sure talking was really a good idea right now. *Maybe after I talk with Zack*, he finally decided, before closing the door to his room.

* * * *

"I'm just so tired of it," David said, twisting his grip around the wheel. He'd still been frustrated about the fight with Charlie when he'd arrived at the Alpha's house, and Jack had picked up on it immediately after getting into the car. He made David tell him the story, and while recapping the whole thing didn't exactly help with the lingering anger, it was a relief to talk to someone about it.

"Man, that sucks." Jack shook his head from the passenger seat. "I'm glad Taylor doesn't pull stuff like this." He paused. "No, wait, he does, but not that often. I guess he started to realize Julia and I grew up while he was gone."

"My brother gets it one minute, then forgets it the next." David grimaced.

"Not cool."

"Yeah."

Jack shrugged. "Julia has it worse than I do, I think, which pisses her off and I don't blame her. My moms and Taylor try not to treat us differently, and they are so careful not to say 'because you're a girl and it's different', that it's sometimes hilarious to watch them squirm, but they still pull something like this every once in a while."

David snorted. "Maybe I should feel lucky I'm not a girl. Charlie would be doing a perfect reenactment of a father with a shotgun on his lap every time I leave the house."

They laughed and most of the tension finally left him. He and Charlie had never fought for long, and David knew they were going to patch things up this time as well—until the next time, of course.

They were almost at the city limits, and aside from the car in the distance coming the other way, there was no one else around. He took a deep breath and decided to just enjoy the rest of the day. And after shopping and dropping Jack off, maybe he'd call Zack and see what he was doing.

Then suddenly the car that was driving their way started swerving on the road and went straight at them. On instinct, David took a sharp turn right, but there was nowhere for him to go, no chance to maneuver. He felt the other car bump into their back right before they collided with a tree.

Chapter Thirteen

Zack and Portia got the car accident call right as they were about to stop for lunch, and Portia groaned.

"No-o-o."

He agreed with the sentiment, but he still radioed in that they would take the call. Rhonda, their dispatcher, told them that there was also ambulance on the way, so Zack pushed the gas pedal a little harder. Hopefully it was just a precaution, but they couldn't be sure.

He almost drove off the road when he recognized David's truck.

"Fuck," he said, pulling the cruiser to the side and getting out as soon as he'd turned off the engine. He saw David leaning against the side of the truck, alive, standing and seemingly fine, but Zack's heart was still lodged in his throat until David looked up and slumped in relief when he noticed him.

"Hey." He leaned into the touch when Zack grasped his arm, probably too hard for someone who was just in a car accident. "I'm fine, but I'm not sure about Jack." He blinked and straightened up. "Jack. I think he may be in shock."

Zack had been a deputy sheriff for a few years now, and he had never hesitated to help anyone. And he would never, ever tell anyone that for half a second — not even that — he hesitated. His wolf, restless and irritated after realizing David had been in danger, did not like the fact that Jack was with him when it happened. Didn't like that at all.

But when David pulled back from him and waved toward the other side of the truck, Zack shook it off and remembered where he was and what he was doing here. He looked around and saw Portia talking with the driver from the other car. Zack couldn't see the driver's face, but he could see the guy was holding a baby in his arms — a baby that was screaming bloody murder.

Then Zack turned and saw Jack leaning against the passenger door on the opposite side of the truck from where Zack and David were. He seemed to be staring at the forest, as if it would give him the answers about what had happened.

Which was what Zack wanted to know as well. The front of David's truck was smashed into the tree and the back was busted on one side. From the way the cars were positioned, the other car had to have caused the dent in the back.

With his blood boiling and no answers, Zack turned to David, who was frowning, glancing between Jack and the other driver with a crying kid.

Then the terrible thought came and Zack heard himself say it out loud before he could stop himself.

"Are you still drunk?" *You can't smell any alcohol*, his brain reminded him a moment later, but he'd known David and Jack were drinking last night —

"What?" David turned to him, eyes wide. "No, of course not."

Zack's nostrils flared. "Then what the hell happened here? How did you drive off the road? The other car bumped you in the back from the side, so…" He drifted off when he saw Portia come over.

Something shut down behind David's eyes and he crossed his arms over his chest before turning to her. "Can I give my statement to you? The deputy here doesn't seem to be interested in hearing it, since he has already made up his mind."

Zack opened his mouth to argue, but Portia nodded at him. "Why don't you try talking to Jack? I've already spoken with Connor, and I'll talk with David here."

He wanted to protest. There was no way he was leaving David's side now. But David didn't look at him anymore, turning away from him pointedly. Portia tilted her head in the direction of Jack and mouthed, "Go."

Zack took a step back then another one. The baby stopped screaming in the background and he glanced there for a second, only to pause. He knew this guy. Then Portia's words registered. *I've already spoke with Connor.* Connor Warsen. The man who'd left Harrington Hills – and Jack – about a year and a half ago was apparently back in town.

Connor nodded at him when he saw him look, and Zack nodded back reflexively. Then he rounded David's car and stood next to Jack, who didn't even glance at him, didn't turn. He seemed frozen like that, shoulders hunched, arms twisted against his stomach. From this angle, Zack couldn't be sure, but when he took a step forward and stood in front of Jack, he confirmed it. Jack's eyes were glassy with tears.

The last remains of the aggravation he'd felt went away at the sight, and Zack clasped his hand gently over Jack's shoulder.

"Do you have any injuries that you know of?" he asked quietly. There was no way he was asking Jack if he was okay, when the answer was staring him in the face.

Jack's lips parted and he blinked a few times. "No," he whispered.

"Does anything hurt?"

"No. But I may still be..." Jack hesitated and swallowed. "I may be in shock. Maybe."

"That would be completely normal," Zack assured him. "An accident can shake a person, regardless of whether anybody was hurt or not."

Jack let out a shuddering exhale that was probably intended to be a snort. "I think something else shocked me more."

As if on cue, the baby wailed again. Jack closed his eyes.

"I get that it's hard on you," Zack said slowly, and he allowed himself only one glance at David as he did. "But I need you to tell me what happened."

"We were going to Linwood, since David wanted to buy bathroom tiles and I offered to help. The road was clear, save for one car driving from the other side. It was fine, then suddenly, when that car was close, it swerved really badly, heading into our lane. David was super quick, but he didn't have anywhere to go. We hit the tree to avoid the collision, but he — But the other car still bumped into us from behind." He put his fist against his lips. "Better than hitting us in the front, I guess."

"Did you drink anything prior to the drive?" Zack made himself ask, even when the memory of David's accusatory look showed up in his head.

"What? No." Jack frowned. "I just told you. It was his car — "

"I heard you. But these are questions I have to ask."

Jack sagged. "No, I didn't drink anything. And neither did David, damn it."

"Were you distracted in any way or —"

"No distractions. We weren't even saying anything right then, and it happened so fast that I barely noticed until David took the sharp turn."

Zack breathed out in relief. "Good." He squeezed Jack's shoulder. "Good."

Before he could say anything else, he heard the ambulance coming. He looked over at Portia, who had just finished taking David's statement. Their eyes met, and she nodded. *It's fine*, she was telling him, but he still couldn't relax. And the distance from David was making his skin itchy. He had to fight the urge to get close, to run his hands over David to check if he was really unharmed.

He wouldn't want to talk to you right now, Zack told himself, but that only made his wolf want to whine. *You're on the job, and there are people around.* He tried the different approach and it worked a bit better.

Zack stood back and watched the paramedics work, but his gaze kept going back to David again and again. David didn't talk with the paramedic long and from what Zack heard — he would use the excuse of work for eavesdropping, because he would go crazy if he didn't hear some positive news right now — David was fine.

Portia appeared next to him. "I took photos of everything we need, so we can get out of here as soon as the medics are done. I'm guessing you want to drive Jack and David back?"

"Yeah." He didn't care how much David protested, Zack was getting him home. "I'm guessing Connor and the baby are getting a trip to the hospital. We need to take care of both cars."

"I've already made the call. The tow will be here soon. I'll stay and catch a ride with them."

Zack glanced at her. "You don't need me around, huh?"

"Not when you're like this, no." Portia bumped her shoulder into his. "But don't worry, you'll buy me lunch and tell me all about what just happened here, and we'll call it even."

"Two lunches and no talking, how about that?"

"Keep it up and it will be two lunches *and* talking."

Zack shut his mouth then and walked over to the front of David's car, staring at the dented metal and broken lights. His stomach turned at the sight. Logically, he knew it wasn't a bad accident, especially not for the werewolves, but he wasn't really using his logic now. He looked up again. David was leaning against the side of the car next to Jack, staring with him at the forest. They didn't seem to be saying anything.

When he glanced at the group gathered next to the ambulance, he noticed Connor turning to look at Jack. Well, at Jack's back. It lasted only two seconds or so, then Connor was focused on the baby again, but, coupled with Jack's reaction, Zack wondered if maybe the whole town had missed it—maybe he'd missed it, maybe these two hadn't been a short-lived fling after all.

You can keep a secret in this town after all, he thought, shaking his head. *Who would've thought*?

When Zack noticed the tow car on the horizon, he walked back to Portia.

"I'm going to take the guys with me now. Call me when you're done here. I should be at the station by then."

She glanced at where David and Jack were still turned away from everyone, then back at Zack. "How about you call me when you're done?"

Zack nodded. "Fine."

He turned and took a deep breath before coming up to where David and Jack were standing.

"Come on. I'll take you both home," he said softly, not wanting to spook either of them.

"Are they gone?" Jack asked, not moving.

Zack opened his mouth to tell him no, but the sound of the door shutting made him turn, and he saw one of the paramedics patting the closed doors on the back of the ambulance then circling it to the driver's seat.

"They're going now."

David didn't say anything, but when Jack straightened up, he did the same. Zack realized he was taking his cues from Jack, letting him lead, and Zack almost felt jealous. He would be, in any other situation, but something in Jack made Zack forget about his feelings. As he watched his cousin blink then slowly turn to walk back to the sheriff's department's cruiser, he wanted to pull the ambulance door open and drag Connor out to kick his ass for whatever he'd done to Jack.

Instead, he reached out right when Jack was about to pass him by and pulled him into a hug. Zack secured his arms around his cousin's body and nuzzled his shoulder with his chin, spreading his scent — pack scent, family scent — over Jack. For a long few seconds it felt as if he was embracing a statue, but then Jack lifted his arms and returned the hug. He sagged into Zack's body with a wet sigh and hid his face in Zack's chest.

They stood like this for a minute before Jack pulled back and, without looking Zack in the eyes, walked the rest of the way to the car. Zack turned and bit his lower lip when he realized David was already in the backseat of the cruiser. It wasn't like Zack had planned to embrace him like he did Jack—*I would have. Given the chance, I would have*—but the way David cut off their contact sent a cold shiver down his spine.

Finally, he nodded at Portia and at the guys just getting out from the tow car, then he got into the cruiser. As he shut the door, he sat back and inhaled the scents of Jack and David, reminding himself they were both safe, as the two crashed cars stood right in front of him.

Zack glanced in the rearview mirror and the question, *Are you okay?* got stuck in his throat again. No, they were not okay.

Neither was he.

Chapter Fourteen

David had never experienced a detachment like this before. He felt as if everything were behind some kind of wall. He didn't seem to care about anything, and the brief flashes of sensations that somehow managed to get through this new, shaky barrier made him wish to make it stronger — the flash of fear when he'd seen the other car coming, the flash of Zack's anger resonating through him like an echo, before coming back out full force, because *how could he?* Then just misery — his, Jack's, his again. The only thing that had made sense was to lean on the car next to Jack and look where he was looking. David wished he could shield him from whatever he needed to be shielded from.

Then there was Zack again. Zack had offered comfort to Jack, and David had almost cried, almost pulled them apart to get there, too, to be given the same treatment. But then he was back behind the wall again, and he hadn't felt anything. He'd relaxed his closed fists and gotten into the back of the cruiser.

David had almost felt something when Zack had looked at him in the rearview mirror, but he'd turned to stare out the window. He'd focused on his breathing and the familiar scent helped his compacted muscles to start relaxing a little.

He was pretty sure that Jack called someone at one point—Taylor, probably. He briefly considered calling Charlie, but after their morning conversation—*had it been just this morning, really?*—David didn't want to talk to him. He wasn't going to be a needy little brother, not when it would only prove Charlie's point.

After a while, they dropped Jack off at his house, straight into the arms of his mothers, and David heard Zack talking to them from the driver's seat, but he didn't register a word they were saying.

Then it was just him and Zack, and David closed his eyes. He could feel his wall slowly disappear and he didn't want that, not now—not before there was at least one real, solid wall between him and Zack.

The car stopped, and he couldn't keep his eyes closed anymore. But when he opened them, Zack didn't seem in any hurry to get out. When their gazes met in the rearview mirror, he just looked at David for a long moment.

"We don't need to leave the car yet," Zack finally said, quietly, as if he didn't want to spook him.

It had an exact opposite effect. David sat up and pulled at the handle. The door was locked.

"Let me out."

Zack did, without saying anything else. Then he got out as well, and followed David to his apartment.

David was lost about what was happening.

"What are you—" he started to ask, but then Zack's arms were around him and he was being pulled against Zack's chest, and damn, *damn*, where was his wall when he needed it?

But there was no wall and Zack was holding him close, and his scent was messing with David's head, because he wanted to bury himself in it, wanted to smell like Zack, smell like they did after sex, their scents mixing with the feeling of contentment and safety.

Suddenly he was clutching at Zack's back and inhaling sharply, again and again. When Zack pulled away, David whined at the loss.

"Calm your breathing, David. Come on," Zack told him, leaning so close that their noses were touching. "Breathe with me. In—and out."

David belatedly realized he'd been halfway to hyperventilating just a moment before. *Great.*

"Sit down. I'll get you some water," Zack said gently. He pushed David down onto the couch and stood before him resting his hands on David's shoulders. He didn't seem in a hurry to leave.

He did pull back in the end then went to the kitchen, and David could hear cabinet doors open and close, then the water running in the sink.

Then Zack was back. He sat close enough that they were pressed together, and David allowed himself to have this, for now. In the back of his head, he was still angry, still hurt, but he would give himself a few minutes of this—Zack's closeness, Zack's touch, Zack's scent.

David wished he didn't need this so much.

"Hey, drink this." Zack handed him the glass, and David did as he was told.

They sat in silence for a few minutes before Zack turned to him and put a hand on his back, making David shiver. He wanted to lean into the touch, but there was something cold in the pit of his stomach now, the feelings from the back of his head coming at him full force.

"I'm so glad you're okay," Zack said right as David pulled back and put about a foot of space between them.

"Just as glad that I was sober, I'm sure," he said and his shoulders tensed as he sat up.

Zack didn't try to move closer. *Good.* "I'm sorry for — I'm sorry for the way I acted back then. I saw it was your car, and I didn't know if you were okay, and I just... I got to you and I should've said anything else that was going through my head back then, but somehow what came out was the worst possible thing."

David put the glass down on the coffee table slowly. "I don't get why it came to you at all."

"I'm a deputy sheriff. We always need to ask these kinds of questions. I just — It just came out wrong."

"You think?"

"I'm sorry. This is all I've got. I'm sorry. I overreacted." Zack reached out his hand, but hesitated before pulling it back.

David didn't know if he was happy or disappointed about that. "I'm fine now," he finally said. "You don't have to —" *Stay. Be here. Feel like you have to be here.*

Zack shook his head. "I don't want to leave you alone." Then he paused and looked away. "Unless you'd prefer to call Charlie..."

That pissed David off again. "I'm not calling anyone."

"You shouldn't be alone right —"

"I'm *not* a child!" *For Moon's sake, it's the theme of the day, apparently.* "Don't treat me like one, either of you."

Zack frowned. "I'm not treating you like a child. And who are you talking about? Charlie?"

"Yes. Yes, I'm talking about Charlie!" David stood up and put some more space between himself and Zack. "I'm tired of being treated like I'm still a kid who doesn't know better."

"David, I swear, I didn't mean it like that, okay? I just didn't want you to be alone because of the possible effects of the accident. You seem like you don't want me around…so I thought of Charlie."

The pause was almost too short to be noticed, but David was unusually attuned to Zack and he heard it. Zack wanted to hear him deny it, hear him say that he wanted for Zack to stay.

But David needed to say something else.

"I told Charlie about us this morning"—he hesitated—"about the fact that we're sleeping together."

Zack suddenly stilled in his seat.

"And?" he finally asked.

"He wasn't happy." David shrugged. "He thinks the age difference is too big, and I told him to mind his own business. Let's just…" He drifted off, because Zack wasn't still anymore. He seemed to almost fold himself in half as if he wanted to— Then the stark, terrible realization hit David. "You agree with him."

Zack didn't even look up at him. David wanted to scream, to hit something. *No. This is not happening.*

He moved to stand right in front of Zack, forcing him to acknowledge him and look up. "Do you think I'm too young for you?"

Zack rubbed both his hands over his thighs. "I—"

"I can't believe this." He took a step back and Zack shot up from his seat.

"It's not— It's eight years, David. It's a lot."

"It's a number! Damn it, it's just a number."

"But when the other number is twenty-two—"

David snorted. "Well, at least I was old enough for you to fuck me. Right? Good for you."

Zack looked as if he'd been punched in the face. It gave David a sick sense of satisfaction. Why should he be the only one hurting?

"It's not like that." Zack folded his hands over his middle as if he was hugging himself. "If you think I just wanted to use you, to sleep with you—"

"Well, what I'm supposed to think?" David shouted, losing patience. "What am I supposed to think when you tell me I'm too young for you? 'Sex is fine, but you're too young for anything more', is that it? Is that why we were hiding it?"

Zack narrowed his eyes. "How's that only on me now? You didn't want to tell anyone either."

"I didn't mind telling people after we figured it out. I don't care what people think, damn it!" David shook his head. "But you do, don't you? You do, and you don't want them to know about us sleeping together."

"And we didn't figure it out, from where I'm standing." Zack threw his hands to his sides. "I don't know how caring about what people think is suddenly such a crime, either, but that isn't my biggest concern."

"Fine." David crossed his arms against his chest. "What is it, then?" *Don't tell me it's my age. Don't tell me it's my age.*

"Do we really need to do this right now? You've just been in an accident—"

"Again with the kid gloves!"

"What do you want from me?" Zack exploded. "For me to tell you the age doesn't matter? I can't. I can't tell you that. I do think you're very young—or I'm too old, or whatever."

David didn't want to hear anything else. "You need to leave." He barely heard Zack's sharp inhale over his loud heart. He wanted to be sick. He wanted Zack gone. He wanted…

The front door opened with a bang then Charlie was standing in the entrance, looking between the two of them before crossing the room and pulling David into his arms.

"Are you okay? I met Taylor and he told me... I tried to call you." He pulled back to look at him and grasped David by the neck. "Are you okay?"

He nodded. "I'm fine. It wasn't anything serious."

Charlie looked at him for a long moment and David refused to acknowledge that his brother's closeness made him feel better. He was still angry at him. He was still angry at Zack, who was standing by and watching the family scene.

David turned to him. "I'm not alone anymore. The nanny is here. You can go now."

For a moment Zack looked like he wanted to protest, but then Charlie moved to face him, and Zack took a step back. He nodded.

"Okay," he whispered. Then he was gone.

David pulled out from his brother's embrace to go to his bedroom. He wanted to run. He wanted to shout. He wanted to curl into a ball and not move for a week.

He took a shower instead and didn't make a sound as he cried.

Chapter Fifteen

'You can go now. You need to leave.'

The words were playing over and over in Zack's head when he was coming down the stairs of David's building, when he was getting into the cruiser, when he was speeding down the street.

'Well, at least I was old enough for you to fuck me. Right?'

Zack wanted to drive and never stop. If he could just cut off everything that held him here, in this town, he would get on his bike and never turn back.

But there was no cutting off anybody or anything, because this desire to escape wasn't him anymore, not really. It had been teenage-Zack's dream — to drive off into the sunset and not care about anything. Even then, he'd been a complete shit at that second part, though.

Now, instead of chasing the sunset, he drove back to the station, since he still had half a shift to get through. He and Portia talked the case over and split the paperwork. With no one really harmed and Connor admitting to being at fault, there wasn't really much for them to do but write it all down.

And that suited Zack's mood just fine, because he didn't want to talk to anyone, didn't want to pretend to joke and have a good time. He wanted to get this done, then hole up in his apartment. Even Portia stopped trying to get him to talk. They just sat there, facing each other, buried in their reports and forms.

Finally, six o'clock came, and he was free to go. Zack almost ran out of the station. He drove around town for a bit, passing by David and Charlie's apartment building and by the house David was working on.

He finally arrived home then dragged himself up the stairs. Once inside, he had to bite his lower lip hard because his place still smelled like David. Zack closed his eyes. It was faint and he knew it wasn't going to last long, but it was there.

It hit him in the shower again—the memory of David's wounded look, the way he'd closed himself off, the longing Zack felt to take him in his arms and never let go, and finally the crushing realization that he couldn't, because now David didn't want him anymore.

'You need to leave.'

His wolf whined and Zack swallowed a lump in his throat. *Maybe it was for the best*, he tried to tell himself. *It would hurt even more later on*.

After he was done in the bathroom, he forced himself to get dressed, to eat something. When he was about to lie down on the couch to stare at the TV and pretend he wasn't thinking about David, someone knocked on his door.

There was a split second when he considered his options—Portia? Charlie? David?—but then he recognized the scent. Taylor.

"Kevin's at work and if I spend five more minutes at home, I'll find Connor and kill him for making my baby brother look like he does right now," his cousin told him by way of a hello, holding up a six-pack of Zack's favorite beer.

"So you're not here for an intervention?" Zack moved aside to let him in before closing the door.

"If you need one, I can do that, too." Taylor's shrug was too casual for Zack to buy it.

He sighed, sitting down on the couch. "Is Kevin really working or did you leave him at home so your mothers and Julia wouldn't go out to kill Connor while you're here?"

Taylor sat next to him. "He's really working. Mom B is handling things at home."

"She doesn't want to kill Connor?"

"Oh, she does, but she doesn't want either of us to go to jail for it." Taylor shrugged again. "I wouldn't be surprised if she was planning how to kill him later on without leaving a trace, but that's a worry for another day. You, though" – Taylor turned to sit sideways on the couch, so he could see Zack better – "need to tell me everything."

Zack took a sip of his beer. "There's –"

"If you tell me there's nothing to tell, I'm going to kick your ass."

"You'd try," Zack threw back, their usual banter coming out as a reflex. They'd been tossing it back and forth for years now, the argument of who would win a fight between them. Zack was bigger and had more strength in muscles, but Taylor was the next Alpha and his power was growing all the time. They'd never tested it, though, and likely never would.

"Jack told me you exploded at David back at the scene," Taylor told him, not willing to take the bait this time.

"I didn't explode. I was... I arrived there and saw his car hit front and back, and I lost it for a moment, okay? Everything was just bubbling out of me and I sensed his anxiety, and"—he rubbed his forehead—"I said the wrong things back there. I know that. But I wasn't thinking straight."

Taylor hummed and nodded. "And what happened after you dropped Jack off?"

'Well, at least I was old enough for you to fuck me, right?' Zack closed his eyes. "I took him home. We fought. He told me to leave, then his brother showed up. I left."

"What did you fight about?"

"He told me he was sick of being treated like a kid. Then he asked if I think he's too young for me."

"And you said yes," Taylor finished with a sigh.

Zack looked at him. "What I was supposed to do? Lie?"

"It's not about lying." Taylor shook his head. "Did he tell you something else?"

Other than to leave? "He thinks that I didn't want to tell anyone about us because of that."

"Because he's too young?"

"Yes."

"And what did you tell him?"

"I"—he shrugged—"I'm not even sure at this point. Whatever I tried to say, he was taking it as me treating him like a kid. Then when I wanted to step back and have that conversation we hadn't had yet—the one where you're supposed to figure things out—his brother showed up."

"Did he figure it out about the two of you?"

Zack snorted, put his beer on the coffee table then ran his hands over his face. "David told him this morning. Charlie wasn't happy, obviously. He used the age argument, and they fought."

"So then when you two fought—"

The age was a hot topic already. "Yeah."

Taylor sat back against the cushions. "Damn..."

"Yeah," Zack repeated, sitting back as well.

There was a moment of silence when Zack stared at his hands on his lap, and Taylor rolled his bottle between his fingers.

"You're not done, though, are you?" Taylor finally asked, and Zack shrugged, feeling his throat close up. "No, no, you're not giving up on this."

Zack looked at him. "I'm not—" he started with a scratchy voice, but Taylor cut him off.

"Do you want to be with him? And not like, meeting up for sex and leaving, but really be with him? Spend time with him? Get to know him better?"

Yes. Yes, yes and yes. Zack closed his eyes. "It's not just about me wanting it."

"It is when we're talking about you fighting for it."

"Are we? Because I don't remember agreeing to this."

"Well, it's happening," Taylor told him bluntly. "I can't have you throwing this away, if you want to be with him."

"Why?"

Taylor gave him a look that said 'you're an idiot'. "Because I want you to be happy? And because I don't want you to keep pretending age is really the biggest issue here."

"I'm not pretending anything."

"But you know this isn't about *David's* age." Taylor put his bottle away. "What do you think about David?"

"In what way?"

"In any way. Just tell me what you think of him."

Zack frowned. He didn't know what Taylor wanted to accomplish here. "He's driven," he started slowly. "He's pro-active—didn't want to sit around and let his brother provide for him, so he started working early. He wanted to pull his weight, and I like that." Zack's gaze was glued to his hands. "He didn't like how he was treated in the jobs he did, so he went out and started his own business. Now he's basically rebuilding a house on his own, which is cool. I can barely hammer a nail into a wall." He shrugged. "He's not afraid. He stands up for himself."

"Not a pushover, huh?"

Zack snorted at that. "No. He's not stubborn just to have his way. He's too laid back for that, but I don't see him taking shit from anybody."

"Good for him." Taylor nodded. "What's the age issue about, then?"

"What?" Zack looked up.

"With everything you told me, what's your issue with his age again? Because not one thing you just told me suggests he is immature or naive."

"He isn't, but he's still twenty-two. You know what I did at his age?"

"Here we go," Taylor commented, but he sounded weirdly…satisfied. It gave Zack a pause.

"What?"

"This is it. This is your problem," Taylor said, resting his arm over the back of the couch. "It's not about David. It's not about how old he is. It's about you and who you were when you were his age."

Zack stared at the floor as he tried to catch his breath. Taylor's words had hit him over the head, and he didn't know what to do, how to react.

"I was a stupid kid back then," he finally whispered.

Taylor nodded. "Actually, at twenty-two you were coming out of it. But even before… Man, you were a rebellious kid. You acted out because you were upset and angry. Sure, you did some stupid things — I won't argue that one — but you were never as bad as you think you were. There are millions of rebellious teenagers out there. You weren't all that special about it."

"It felt special for Harrington Hills," Zack muttered, and Taylor snorted.

"Okay, I'll give you that. You were the most rebellious kid back then. But you know there were more kids like you. You know there are kids like that now, too. None of you had done things that couldn't be fixed. And you grew out of it, damn it. You became a freaking pillar of the community with your uniform and cool badge and all." Taylor smirked.

"Yeah, but that's now," Zack said, ignoring the tease. "David's twenty-two and he has all these things figured out."

Taylor shook his head. "You think you're somehow worse because you started doing what you're doing a few years later than a kid who lost both his parents and had to learn to take care of himself with only his brother there to help? If that's your example of how things should go, most of us would fall short, I can tell you that."

"Well, what about you? When you were that age, you were almost all groomed and ready to become — "

"What's with you and this putting yourself down bullshit?" Taylor cut him off. "You've always been so sure I have everything figured out."

"Because you have!" Zack twisted to face Taylor. "You were always this poster child of the pack. You knew where you were headed, and you did everything right. Now you're back in town with your mate, whom everyone likes, and you fit right in as if you'd never left. I'm happy for you — I am — but you're not exactly a good example of not having things figured out."

Taylor looked away for a long moment and rubbed his ear. He sighed. "Okay, listen. I'm going to tell you something that you can't—absolutely can't—tell anyone else about, all right?" When Zack nodded, he continued. "So, here's the thing. When I first came home with Kevin—for Amanda and Terry's wedding—we weren't a couple."

Zack stared at him. "What?"

Taylor chuckled humorlessly. "My mother had told me a few weeks before the wedding that if I came alone, she was going to set me up with someone—or multiple someones." He shook his head. "She'd decided that she was tired of me dragging my feet. And I'd hated the idea. Hated it. The thought of coming home only to have to fight off her match-making... Well, long story short, I'd asked Kevin to pretend to be my date. He thought I was crazy, and I don't blame him, but he'd agreed."

Zack tried to understand what he was hearing, but it was hard. He remembered picking them up from the airport. They'd seemed— "So wait. When did you—?"

"Around the time of the wedding." Taylor rubbed his ear again. "Listen. I can joke about it now—Kevin and I both do sometimes—but the truth is, I almost blew it." He stared at his arm resting over the back of the couch. "I don't know if I'd have ever realized who he was to me if we hadn't done it, if he hadn't come with me. Maybe I would, maybe I wouldn't, but the chance that I might not have scares the shit out of me, not to mention that I almost pushed him away while we were here." He looked straight at Zack. "Listen. The point is, you're so sure other people have everything figured out while you're somehow behind on everything. And I don't know, maybe some people do have their shit together right from the start, but that's not the majority of us. It definitely wasn't me."

Zack nodded, but he was still digesting everything, and Taylor seemed to pick up on that. He nodded and got up.

"I'll get us another beer."

You do that, Zack wanted to say, but he was still stuck on the thought of Taylor and Kevin…

'I almost blew it.'

Damn.

Zack closed his eyes and David's face was right there under his eyelids, a stark reminder of everything he might have already lost.

Chapter Sixteen

When David woke up the next morning, he decided there was no way he was leaving the apartment. The house could wait, especially since they hadn't made it to the store yesterday. He was taking the day off.

He dragged himself to the kitchen before Charlie could get an idea to maybe call in to work and take the day off as well. They hadn't talked much last night after Zack had left and David had holed himself up in his room. Charlie had let him be, only knocking once right before bed to make sure he was okay. David, buried under his covers and replaying the fight with Zack over and over in his head, had lied through his teeth when he told his brother he was fine.

"Hey," he told him now, after entering the kitchen.

"Hey." Charlie watched from his seat at the table as David poured himself coffee. "How are you feeling?"

David shrugged. "I'm fine. I didn't get hurt. I didn't hit my head or anything."

"You're not going to the house, are you?"

Charlie's question made him want to do the exact opposite of what he'd planned, but he resisted. "I'm not. But we'll have to take your car to the store on Saturday. I don't know how long my truck's going to be out."

"Okay, sure." Charlie looked at him carefully when David sat down at the table. "I can drive by the mechanic to find out?" It sounded more like a question than Charlie's usual way of announcing things, and David appreciated that.

"Great, thanks."

They didn't touch on any tricky topics, but David was still on edge, and when Charlie finally left, he breathed out in relief. He was free to do whatever.

As it turned out, he couldn't sit still, even when there was a part of him that wanted to bury himself under the blankets and never get up. He tried that, but rolled out of bed twenty minutes later.

He was about to do laundry when there was a knock on the door.

David's heart started going faster. *Zack*, it told him, but he just shook his head. *No. No wishful thinking.*

But as he was nearing the door the faint scent of Zack made his heart stutter and his stomach turn. David slowly walked the rest of the way to the entrance. *Calm down*, he told himself before opening the door and coming face to face with Zack.

"Hey." Zack was the first one to break their staring contest. He looked down at the ground. "Can we talk?"

David wanted to nod and pull him in, bury himself in Zack's chest and forget about yesterday. But he curled his arms around his chest instead and made himself ask, "Do you think we have anything else to talk about?"

"I hope so." Zack glanced up at him. "I know I have things I'd like to say, and I'm open to hearing anything you'd want to tell me. But it's up to you now."

It's up to you now. If it were truly up to him, they wouldn't need this now, whatever *this* was. But there was a part of him that was pleased Zack had given him the lead.

"Come in." David stepped aside and gestured him to the couch when Zack paused in the entrance. "Come on. We're not doing it standing here."

"How are you feeling?" was Zack's first question and David repeated what he'd told Charlie. If Zack was asking for anything more than his physical state, he'd have to be more specific.

Zack took a deep breath. "We didn't get to— I didn't get to say everything I wanted to say yesterday. And it's mostly good that I didn't, because I'd have messed it up, but I also wish... I wish I hadn't left you thinking that I didn't care. That I don't care."

David stared at a point behind Zack's shoulder. He couldn't make himself look Zack in the eyes as he tried to hold himself together. He didn't want to let himself hope. He didn't want to—

"I noticed you right away, and I've never stopped noticing you," Zack said quietly, and when David glanced at him, he saw Zack's gaze was fixed on his knees. "I might have been fighting it, but I've been interested in you ever since you put the first plank on the ground."

"You've been fighting it." David looked away at the wall, disappointed. He was going to hear the same old song again.

Zack nodded. "I did. I'm not here to lie to you about it. I've been fighting it, because I wasn't interested in a fling or a flirt that led nowhere, and I was sure a guy like you wouldn't want anything serious with me."

"A guy like me?"

"Young and very attractive."

David shook his head, but before he could say anything, Zack continued.

"Then, on the full moon, my wolf didn't want to step away from you after the welcoming. I wanted to stay and keep scenting you, and just...be with you. But we barely knew each other and the entire pack was there, so I pulled myself away."

"I wanted you to stay then too," David admitted quietly.

Zack ran his hands over his thighs. "I couldn't tell you no later on, when you asked me out. I had all these reasons why I should, but I just couldn't. And these reasons kept losing again and again in my head. I just wanted to spend time with you. The reasons were there, at the back of my mind, but when we were together, they would disappear, only to come back when I was alone. I know now that some of them are stupid, but—"

"The age thing is definitely stupid," David told him. Whatever else bothered Zack, David could deal with. But he wasn't budging on this.

"The age thing is..." Zack hesitated. "It's my issue, and Taylor helped me realize it last night. Now I feel like an idiot to dump it on you."

"Okay, but what is it? What's so bad about being younger?"

"I was a stupid kid when I was your age," Zack said slowly, "and you aren't. You're probably more mature than I am right now, but I didn't know that at the start. I just assumed no one your age would want anything serious. Then I did know you better and instead of being happy you're not like I used to be, I started to compare us. I came up short every time."

"On what?" David shook his head with disbelief. "Like, seriously? On what are you coming up short, because I don't see it. And I don't get why we even need that measuring contest anyway."

Zack offered him a half-smile. "See? You're smarter than me."

"Shut up." David smacked his knee before looking down at his hand. Zack brought his slowly closer and twined his fingers with David's.

"I'm sorry for the way I made you feel," Zack went on, looking straight at him now. "With the secrecy and dumping my issues on you —"

"I think I dumped some of mine on you, too," David admitted. "The age thing is my problem, too. It's just different than yours."

"And I should've known, because you told me — about Charlie, about the bosses that refused to see your worth because you were young. I should've known."

David took a deep breath. He didn't want to let himself hope, but... "Well, you do know now. We both do. What's next?"

Zack squeezed his fingers. "I would like to ask you out on a date, if you still want to do this. You pick the place."

David bit his lip. "And if I pick a place in the middle of the town?"

"Whatever you want," Zack told him, his thumb running over David's knuckles. "I don't care if people see us. I don't enjoy the gossip, but it will be worth it."

"Are you sure?"

"Yes."

David let out a shaky breath. This seemed too good to be true. "So you want to date me?"

"I do. I want to date you and, if things go right, I want us to stay together. I don't have an escape plan or an exit strategy, if you're worried about that. Sure, we still…we still may not work out, for whatever reason, but I hope we do."

It was good enough for David. He couldn't wait any longer. He leaned in and kissed Zack, pouring everything he was feeling — good and bad — into it. Because this was what he wanted — them, together, handling both good and bad. He didn't want an exit strategy either. He didn't plan on needing one.

Zack pulled back. "Wait."

"What?" David was about to straddle Zack, so he sat back on his haunches.

"Yesterday, you said something…" Zack grimaced and backed away even more until his back was against the couch arm rest. "You said, '*at least I was old enough for you to fuck me*' and that's — I just want to make sure that you know that's not all there is in it for me. I think you're incredibly hot and you know that, obviously, but I don't… I don't want you to think it's all about sex for me. Or, worse, that it's all about sex with someone much younger."

David ran a hand through his hair. "I know that. And I'm sorry about what I said. That was out of line — "

"No, it wasn't — "

"Yes, it was." David put a hand over Zack's mouth to stop him from talking. When their gazes met again, David felt happier than he had been since the last time he'd left Zack's bed. "It's obvious that it's completely the opposite thing for you. So, no, I'm not worried you want me for my young body, okay?"

Zack nodded and licked David's palm that was still covering his mouth. David laughed and moved both hands to the back of Zack's neck and leaned over him for another kiss.

They might get a proper shot at this thing after all.

Epilogue

Two weeks later

Zack smiled, coming out of the dream, as the first things he registered were kisses across his collarbone. "Hi, there," he murmured without opening his eyes, and David huffed a laugh right into his chest.

"Hi."

"Don't stop on my account." Zack brought his hand to rest at the back of David's neck.

He got bitten on a nipple a moment later, but that was hardly a punishment. He kept his mouth shut, though, enjoying the sensations. David kept moving down his body slowly, and by the time he reached his destination, Zack's cock was hard and waiting for him.

Zack opened his eyes at the first lick of David's tongue over the head of his cock, because he couldn't miss a view like that. The way David looked, his lips sealed around Zack's erection, was the best damn sight to wake up to.

He squeezed David's neck and ran his thumb back and forth behind David's ear, making him moan around Zack's cock. "Yeah, that's so good," Zack said.

David sped up his movements, moving up and down, then licking around the head. He'd already discovered a few things that had made Zack crazy, and he used them to his advantage now. Then David grasped the base of Zack's cock and started to jack him off in the same rhythm he was moving his mouth and tongue.

Zack arched up into it, but David just pushed him down, and Zack threw his head back, feeling his orgasm near.

"Gonna come," he whispered to be polite, even if he knew damn well David didn't care about his politeness. He just sucked harder and didn't stop until Zack came down his throat and shivered through aftershocks. And even then, David pulled back only to bury his nose in Zack's pubes and let out a long exhale, tickling him.

"Stop it," Zack chuckled, pulling him up by the neck and licking into his mouth when David moved up his body. Tasting himself on his mate's lips didn't seem to be getting old.

Mate. Two days ago the word had first appeared in his head and he'd almost dropped the coffee he'd been holding. Now it seemed more right than anything else when he thought about David. He hadn't said it out loud yet, though. His mind was telling him it was too soon, too quick. His heart wanted him to scream it at the top of his lungs in the middle of a crowd.

As a compromise, he promised himself he'd say it soon. He just had to pick the right moment.

David pulled back a little and raised one eyebrow. "Where did you go?"

"Nowhere." Zack leaned in and bit his jaw gently, playfully. Then he reached down and closed his fingers around David's erection. "We have some unfinished business here."

"You bet your ass we do," David said, but his voice was already lower as he pushed into Zack's grip.

Zack smirked. "You don't really need me to do much, do you?" He tightened his grip and David rested his forehead against his shoulder.

"Fuck," David breathed out quietly, working himself toward an orgasm as he moved back and forth.

Zack grasped one of David's ass cheeks with his free hand and pushed him forward harder. "Come on," he whispered with his lips right above David's ear. "Come all over me, so everybody can smell it, even after I shower."

Zack grinned as David came with a full-body shudder. He knew a few tricks of his own, too.

He was still grinning when David moved off him to lie by his side. They stared at the ceiling for a minute or two.

"So," David said, and Zack could tell he was grinning too. "Full moon run tonight."

"Yeah."

It wasn't the first pack event they'd spent together — there had been a picnic in the park last weekend — but the first full moon run was somehow almost as special. Neither of them had shifted since the night of the Joining Ceremony, and Zack wanted to feel that connection again, this time knowing that he could take all the time he wanted scenting David — mixing their scents.

He couldn't wait.

About the Author

Megan is one of those people who dreamed of being a writer since they were a little kid and then didn't do anything about it for years. Then as a teenager she was introduced to fandom and…well. She fell head first into it and never looked back. At some point she decided to try writing her own characters in her own stories. And that's where she is today.

When she's not writing, Megan works as a psychologist and continues to learn the hard way that she can't give all her clients their happy ending (she truly believes everyone can save themselves, though). That's why she makes sure to give it to her characters, always.

She loves TV shows, books, fanworks and pizza (not necessarily in that order). But there's nothing like getting messages from readers who enjoy her stories, so if you're not sure it's okay to contact her—yes, it is.

Megan loves to hear from readers. You can find their contact information, website details and author profile page at http://www.pride-publishing.com.